Lucy Fricke was born in Hamburg in 1974. After working in the film industry for several years, she studied creative writing at the prestigious Leipzig Literary Institute. She has published four novels in the past twelve years, winning her a number of awards including the 2018 Bavarian Book Prize for *Daughters*. Lucy Fricke has been running HAM.LIT since 2010, the first Hamburg festival for upcoming literature and music. She was a resident at the German Academy in Rome and at Ledig House, New York. A member of German PEN and a founding member of the Kook artists' and writers' network, she has judged both the Friedrich Luft Prize for theatre productions and the Karl Heinz Zillmer Prize for publishers. She lives in Berlin.

Sinéad Crowe comes from Dublin. After completing a PhD in German theatre at Trinity College Dublin and working for several years as a lecturer in German Studies, she moved to Hamburg, where she began her career as a translator. Her translations include Ronen Steinke's *Fritz Bauer: The Jewish Prosecutor Who Brought Eichmann and Auschwitz to Trial* and Pierre Jarawan's *The Storyteller*, a co-translation with Rachel McNicholl. Sinéad Crowe also teaches at the University of Hamburg's Institute of English and American Studies.

Daughters

Lucy Fricke

Translated from the German by Sinéad Crowe

V&Q BOOKS

The translation of this work was supported by a grant from the Goethe-Institut in the framework of the 'Books First' programme.

V&Q Books, Berlin 2020
An imprint of Verlag Voland & Quist GmbH
Originally published under the title TÖCHTER
Copyright © 2018 by Rowohlt Verlag GmbH, Reinbek bei Hamburg, Germany
All rights reserved
Translation copyright © Sinéad Crowe
Editing: Katy Derbyshire
Copy editing: Alyson Coombes
Cover design: Pingundpong*Gestaltungsbüro
Typesetting: Fred Uhde
Printing and binding: PBtisk, Příbram, Czech Republic
Quoting from 'L'italiano', lyrics by Cristiano Minellono

www.vq-books.eu

Daughters

The Eye of God

I'd been stuck there for three days. Rats scurried through the alleys at night, tourists amassed around the Trevi Fountain during the day. Security guards with machine guns outside the museums, dark underground stations where the filth couldn't be seen, just smelled, and if I wanted to visit the Vatican, I had to book online.

I was staying at the Babylon, a budget hotel staffed entirely by Koreans. Maybe it was because I hadn't planned on coming to Rome, but I fell in love instantly. I'd always had a quiet admiration for places and people that run to seed with their heads held high, so sure of their beauty that they don't give a damn what the rest of the world thinks. It was a desolate diva, this city, utterly foul; the only thing it kept clean was its churches, while outside, pigeons shat on every monument.

I'd only intended to pass through. To go from the airport to Anagnina, the last stop on the metro, and to take a bus from there to a town in the mountains where there was someone I'd been meaning to visit for ten years. He knew nothing about my plans, and he wouldn't have cared anyway, being long dead. But you have to say goodbye to everyone, even the dead, especially the dead, and I'm afraid I had an unhealthy attachment to this man, basically worshipped him. It was liable to become a problem at some point, the way everything becomes a problem at some point, especially love, especially men.

So I'd been making my way, after ten years it was time to start making my way, I'd decided, but now here I was, stuck. On the day I arrived, I stood at the bus station watching people boarding this contraption they call a pullman, a contraption that always seemed to be running late, that had been trundling the streets for decades with the last few rows of seats missing, the windscreen wipers too. But I'd once spent days being carted through a jungle on the bed of a pickup, I'd boarded a rickety propeller plane in howling winds, and I'd ridden pillion on a motorbike while the rider was on the wildest acid trip of his life, as he informed me mid-journey, turning his head to give me a lingering look. Fear was not one of my more prominent traits. So why couldn't I leave this city? Was I lazy, stoic or just a coward when it came to accepting realities, truths I didn't like, truths such as the death of this man?

I was pondering this as I stared up into the Pantheon's dome, into the middle of the hole, into the grey sky over Rome, into the eye of God. A few metres away, a pink helium balloon had got stuck, one of those balloons that were being handed out outside every Victoria's Secret in the city at the time. An ad for fucking underwear was stuck in the dome of the Pantheon, and with every waft of air it danced a little towards the exit, towards freedom. Hundreds of degenerates were transfixed by this spectacle, all eyes on the pink balloon, phone videos recording, and when it finally floated out into the Roman sky, the crowd clapped and cheered as if the Messiah had just appeared.

My bag began to vibrate just as a stern 'Quiet please' came from the loudspeaker in four languages. I answered anyway, and Martha was on the other end.

'Where are you?' she asked.

I glanced up at the ceiling as if to double-check. 'I'm in the Pantheon.'

'You answered your phone in a church?'

'It's not a church, it's the most godawful tourist trap on the planet. We're packed in like sardines – I wouldn't be able to get out even if I tried.'

'Please do try,' Martha said in a low voice. 'I need to talk to you alone for a minute, somewhere quiet.'

'I'm in Rome. They don't do "alone" here,' I said as I tried to find a route through the masses.

'What on earth are you doing in Rome?'

'Nothing. I just thought, you know, everyone should visit Rome at least once.'

'You're getting odder.'

'Well, at least my crises are getting more refined as I get older,' I replied. 'We're having a rare old time right now, my crisis and me.'

I passed the biggest door I'd ever seen in my entire life. It was at least six metres high and made of bronze. If the doors of heaven are anything like that, I'll never get in.

'Still there, Martha?'

What followed was a dangerously weak 'Yes'. I'd never heard her sound so weak before. There was something so ominous about this 'yes' that I didn't hesitate for a second. I didn't ask any questions. We'd known each other for long enough now to recognise when one of us was about to crack. Martha would start to cry on the phone, and crying on the phone is even worse than crying alone in the back of a taxi. You can't clutch on to someone on the phone; a voice is less than a little finger. I would fly back right away.

Just as I was hanging up, a pigeon shat on my head. I'd learned by now that this wasn't a good omen.

All Sorted

I'd taken the first flight out, the night so short as to be practically non-existent, and now, at around half past nine on a Monday morning, I was dragging my suitcase across Warschauer Bridge, where the party had just broken up, the revellers either in bed, passed out in a pool of vomit or still dancing in some club. I trudged past empty bottles of cheap sparkling wine, shattered beer bottles and an abandoned amp. Shards crunched beneath the wheels of my case. Around the next corner, right beside a massive building site, was my flat. The stairwell smelled like an exploded beer cellar, and a numb silence had taken hold. The building had adapted to its bacchanalian surroundings. To survive the noise here, you needed a country retreat or a job abroad. To afford the rent, you had to sublet your rooms to people from duller countries, people who came here to behave in ways they would never dream of at home. We lived in a muddle, sleeping on sofas with the downstairs and upstairs neighbours, while in our own flats, party tourists pissed on the parquet floors.

I financed myself by fleeing the city. Whenever I was strapped for cash, I would head to parts of the world that were cheaper than this one, of which there were many. 'Kill the investor in you,' I'd read on the side of a building in Kreuzberg recently and cheerfully disregarded. I felt that I'd been living in this neighbourhood long enough now to deserve a piece of the pie, that in fact I myself was the pie. So, like nearly everyone else, I flogged my own home for 80 euros a night.

And then on Thursdays we'd clutch our cardboard coffee cups at demos to save the Turkish greengrocer's, if not the entire neighbourhood, from being driven out, standing alongside artists from Charlottenburg and Prenzlauer Berg who'd shown up to express their solidarity and day-trippers carrying canvas bags emblazoned with protest slogans. A few speeches, a few songs about the rising rents and the selling-out, and demand on Airbnb would shoot up another twenty per cent. The tourists bought the bags and later toted them around New York, Barcelona and Lower Bavaria. No one ever bought vegetables.

The face in my mirror looked exactly as old as it was: just over forty. The lines stayed white in the sun now, as if I'd shattered on the inside. I could only call myself beautiful in the past tense. Age had arrived by night, and it kept on coming. I used to grow while I dreamt, but soon I would start shrinking in my sleep, waking up smaller each morning until I vanished entirely. Sometimes I wondered how I was going to get through all the time until then. And to top it all off, there was more hair sprouting on my face each day.

The Spanish kid had thrown up next to my toilet, the stereo had been set to the highest volume. A jar of peanut butter, a chunk of Emmental and a bottle of beer in the fridge, three cigarette butts stamped out on the floor. *José, 24, lives in Madrid.* The picture in my bedroom was now hanging upside down. Apparently José was a practical joker. I was glad I'd never met him.

It took me two hours to clean the flat, to purge it, to scrape Spanish youth out of the cracks. When I was done, I opened José's beer, sat down by the window and looked out at the Spree. It was mid-April and the river was still a river rather than a party strip. In less than six weeks, the techno cruisers would be blaring past, their lasers groping the walls of my study. I'd be looking out at frenzied stag and hen parties, at semi-clad men and even less-clad women, all of whom would be thinking they were having the time of their lives and would probably be right, a state of affairs I found increasingly pitiful.

There was no sign of Martha when I arrived at the bar. There was no sign of anyone, apart from a barman I'd never seen before, who was polishing glasses. Martha had suggested the location, a former haunt of hers, though whether this was for sentimental reasons or for lack of a better idea, I didn't know. It felt like a lifetime since we'd spent our nights here with Henning, a boyfriend she would regularly resolve to leave, only to eventually marry him last year. And with Jon, Henning's oldest friend, whom we hadn't been able to save, who'd made this bar his favourite and only companion, leaving his money and his will to live at the counter until both were gone. I didn't think about Jon very much any more. We rarely talked about him, but then all three of us had got quieter in general since he died. Whether this reticence was down to our age or our pain, whether there was any difference between the two, I wasn't sure. We just kept going, and it wasn't as hard to keep going as we'd expected.

I glanced over at the door just as Martha slipped in, like a shadow. She gave my shoulder a listless stroke and sat down with a groan. She barely looked at me, just at the bottles on the shelves.

Martha only went out these days when it was absolutely necessary, and this necessity always came from within, never from the outside world. It had been a long time since she'd shown any interest in the outside world. She'd been pregnant again and again over the past year: four weeks, six, eight, and afterwards, after the miscarriages, we'd go drinking before it all started up again. I was a little unnerved by the way she emerged from these hormonal torture sessions virtually unchanged. Martha was the toughest old bird I knew. During her unfertilised weeks, she'd always order the most expensive booze, usually neat.

In for a penny, in for a pound, she'd say, and be pissed by her third glass. This was one change that did bother me. At first, I'd felt betrayed. At this age, this stage of life, a stage I couldn't relate to, I had fewer and fewer friends who could stay upright on a barstool beside me. My nights were as long as other people's days. Our lives were out of sync. Hardly anyone ever crossed my path, and the few who did scared me: they were lost souls who latched on to me, sinking their teeth into the backs of my legs.

Martha ordered an eighteen-year-old double whisky before turning to me, exhausted. We hadn't seen each other in over a month, hadn't spoken. This wasn't unusual. I was always out, she was always at home, and we no longer needed reassurance that we were thinking of each other. We were there for each other and we'd stay there. We sat together in silence, like old men in a pub by the factory gate. I ordered myself a beer, a large one. It looked like it was going to be a long, quiet night.

'Why Rome?' she asked eventually.

'No reason really,' I lied. 'Just, every couple of years I think it might help if I found religion. So I spend a day going from church to church, imagining how much better it would all be if I believed in God. I sit there, surrounded by the quiet, the darkness, the damp coldness, the crosses and frescoes on the walls, all that devout suffering, and it feels like maybe everything does have meaning after all. I sit and sit, for hours sometimes, because I know that as soon as I leave, everything will fall apart again.'

'So you went to Rome to sit in a church?'

'Well, where else do you get so many churches, each one better than the one before, a Caravaggio in every corner? If you chuck a euro in the machines, the light goes on and you can actually see the Caravaggio. Plus, I finally understand nuns now. Jesus looks completely different in Italy. Not the emaciated, anguished bloke we have here. No, the man on the cross over there has a six-pack. It's plain lascivious. Anyone would join a convent for a man like that.'

I kept blathering on to give her time. Anyway, I didn't want to talk about the real reason for my trip. Something about it embarrassed me, especially tonight. Tonight wasn't supposed to be about me.

She ordered another whisky, still saying nothing.

'What's up, Martha?'

'First tell me what you were really up to in Rome, apart from drooling over Jesus.'

'I wasn't up to anything in Rome. I'd planned to go to Bellegra, an hour south of the city,' I admitted.

She looked at me in puzzlement.

'I wanted to visit my father's grave.'

'Your father died?'

'Not him. The other one.'

'You've got so many fathers I never know which one you're talking about.'

Martha was exaggerating. There were basically only three. The good one, also known as 'The Trombonist'; the bad one, AKA 'The Prick'; and the biological one, 'Jochen'. My mother and I had vanished from the last one's life so early that he was more like a nice-enough uncle I was always on my best behaviour with. Every now and then, I'd meet up with him for dinner. I'd never been able to feel anything other than pity for him. Not even after my mother wedded The Prick, who in the space of two years wreaked enough havoc on my prepubescent psyche to lumber me with an impressive range of lifelong psychological and sexual defects. The only beacon of hope in this male netherworld was The Trombonist. A gambling-addicted Italian, a devastatingly handsome macho, he'd put me on his shoulders and carried me through the good half of my childhood. I'd loved him to distraction.

'The Trombonist,' I said.

'And he's buried in Bellegra?'

'That's where he was from.'

'Did he ever take you there?'

'No, he never wanted to go back.'

'I'm sorry,' she said.

'Yeah, it's a shame.'

'No, I'm sorry for keeping you from going there now, I mean.'

'I kept myself from visiting for ten years, plus another three days in Rome. That's one good thing about a grave: it waits.'

'Yeah,' Martha said, staring into her glass. 'Yeah. That's why I phoned. Kind of. My father.' She took a large slug. 'My father is a fucking bastard.'

'I know,' I said. 'You've mentioned that.'

For the first thirty years of Martha's life, her father's defining characteristic had been that he was never around, even when she needed him. Especially when she needed him. The stories she'd told me about her childhood were appalling. This father was a kick in the teeth. Her mother had left him early in their marriage, after which he'd taken to the bottle for a few years before getting remarried and then, over the course of this second marriage, almost entirely forgetting about Martha. Our childhood stories were similar in that respect, though our methods of dealing with them were completely different. Now, after several failed attempts to outrun her past, Martha was determined, come hell or high water, to start her own family. She wanted to make it all better, to make something, anything, to be happy, to get on with it. But my childhood, and to an even greater extent my teenage years, had stamped out any desire for a family so thoroughly that the slightest prospect of one made me break out in a cold sweat.

A few years ago, now old and widowed, Martha's father started phoning her once a week. Twice a week after his cancer diagnosis. She'd probably spent a thousand hours on the phone to him since then, she said, and five of them had actually been worth it. There'd been discussions, truths and apologies, even declarations of love. On his part, needless to say.

He wasn't such a bad guy really, Martha had once told me. After all, he hadn't had it easy either. Once you knew where someone came from, which battles they'd won and, more importantly, which they'd lost, the channel opened and love flowed through.

The problem was, where did you go from there? Once everything had been said? You sat around with things nicely cleared up, drinking beer and nattering about politics. With a bit of luck, you could enjoy the odd comfortable silence.

'All he cares about is himself, right to the end,' Martha said. 'But what's really galling is that he wants me to help. Yesterday morning he phones and says, "It's all sorted," something like that. "I've sealed the deal," he says, "they gave me the green light." Then it's, "Princess," and "one last favour." And, "I know you won't let your sick old father down." I mean, sure, who can refuse a last favour? At least you know that'll be the end of it.'

I didn't understand what she was trying to tell me.

'He wants to die, Betty. And he wants me to drive him.'

'What do you mean, drive him?'

'To Switzerland. The appointment is next week.'

'An appointment? Just like that?'

'It's not just like that. He obviously sent them his documents months ago: MRI scans, diagnoses, everything. Joined this organisation, shelled out a small fortune. That's why he's constantly scrounging money off me. All this time I've been wondering why he keeps running out. I just thought he was drinking too much, now I find out he was using my money to fund his death. I mean, how fucked up is that? It's not enough to get his own daughter to pay for him to die, but he expects me to drive him there too.'

While nearly all our friends were inheriting houses, or at least halves of houses, while they droned on over dinner about wills and inheritance tax, Martha, who'd spent years helping her father out of various 'tight spots', as he called them, would just sit there with a bland smile. You never escape your parents' poverty, the smell sticks to you. Even the way you walk betrays everything, so straight, stiff and proud, defying all oppression, lacking all ease.

'And he never let on? What's he been telling you all this time?' I asked.

'He didn't want to be a burden. That's what he says after dropping his bombshell. "I didn't want to be a burden, princess."'

Martha took a cigarette out of my pack, something she only did these days when she was plastered or at her wits' end, usually both, and smoked it in her own special way: staring into nothingness, inhaling deeply, pondering. Martha set herself deadlines for everything, including thinking. By the time she stubbed out this cigarette, she would have made a decision. For particularly difficult decisions, she would buy a cigar. I placed my pack beside her glass.

'No thanks,' she said. 'One's enough.'

Her eyebrows drew together. I knew what this meant for me. Buried in the furrow on her forehead was a request, something she found hard to say, something she didn't know how to put into words. Eventually I took the smoked filter from her hand.

'I can't do it,' she said. 'I can't even drive any more. I can't face it: my father in the passenger seat, our last few hours together.'

Martha hadn't been behind the wheel of a car since the accident. An accident all four of us survived, or so we thought at first, but which changed everything. Which carved up Jon's face and in fact did cost him his life in the end. Martha wouldn't let anyone talk her out of the blame, even though it wasn't her blame to take, and eventually she'd asked Henning and me to stop trying.

'Can't Henning drive?' I asked.

'Henning can't stand my father, you know that. He'd have to bite the steering wheel to keep from screaming at him for the entire journey.'

'I see,' I said.

'Anyway, I couldn't do that to my father.'

'Do what?'

'Henning.'

'But you're married – happily, even. You want to have a baby together. And anyway, Henning's the best.'

At least that's what I'd come to believe. For the simplest of reasons: because he loved Martha. In a way, he had decided on her, a woman without equal, and in the end, that's all love is: a decision.

'My father thinks he's a loser.'

'Come on, Martha, that's not true. Maybe it would be good for the three of you to go together.'

'No!' Martha's voice had got louder. 'You have to come.'

I'd only met Martha's father once, more than ten years ago, and all I remembered about him was a sweaty handshake.

'We'll drive him there, he'll take his dose, and then we'll drive back home,' Martha said.

'Without him?'

'They take care of everything, he said, repatriation and all that.'

Even if everything was exactly the way Martha had described it, I couldn't picture it. How did you drive someone to the place where they would die? What were you supposed to talk about on the way? What were you supposed to eat? Was he even able to eat? Was it okay to listen to music? To enjoy the scenery? What the hell was it okay to do during someone's final days and hours?

Martha started to cry. Just out of her left eye; her right eye remained dry. She could only cry out of one eye. As long as I'd known her, she'd been a left-eyed bawler.

When I put my arm around her, I could feel how rigid she was. It was as though she hadn't exhaled in hours, as though she'd decided to hold her breath until it was all over.

'He wants to go before the pain gets too bad. We'd probably do the same,' I said. I myself was the queen of the disappearing act, someone who would travel halfway round the world to forestall any kind of pain, though in my case the pain was never physical. My body was in enviably good health.

'But he ought to stick around,' she said. 'Phone me every day until he keels over. He ought to at least meet his grandchild, it can't be much longer now. Doesn't he want to see what happens to us all? He can't just say, "I've seen enough now, thanks very much."'

'Yes, he can,' I said.

She nodded.

'Sometimes I wish he was still the shitty father he was for most of my life. Go to hell where you belong, I could say, and send a wreath to his funeral. Deciding to be nice shortly before the end, that's just cruel.'

'Have you told him this?'

'Of course not.'

'I mean that you'd like him to stick around.'

'"Don't try to stop me," he said, but of course I did try. I started crying, he started crying, and then he hung up. Ten minutes later I got a text message with the appointment, nothing else. He's no good at texting.' Martha slumped on her stool.

'But say I did manage to stop him, then I'd be responsible for everything that happens afterwards. And not much good would happen, that's for sure. He'd be in pain, and it'd be my fault.'

She stared into her glass.

'When's the appointment?' I asked.

'Thursday,' she said. 'At two. We'll have to pick him up in Hanover and then drive him down in his car. It's an ancient Golf, but he insists on driving his own car. I mean being driven in it. He can't drive any more. The car's been parked one street over for more than a year now.'

'Can't we take your car?'

'He's dead set on going in his car. You know how it is: memories, nostalgia, all the places he's been in the car, all the people who've sat in it. That car is his buddy. He used to pay it a visit every few weeks, get in and have a beer with it. So if we're going, we're going in his car.'

'Petrol or diesel?' I asked.

'What difference does that make?' Martha looked at me in bafflement.

'I like to focus on the practicalities.'

'Petrol. I think.'

'Four-door?'

'Christ, Martha, yes, and it has a boot too. Like I said, it's a Golf.'

The thought of making one's final journey in a Golf depressed me. I ordered a second pint and a shot.

'Where exactly in Switzerland is it?'

'In Chur,' Martha said. 'Around 800 kilometres from Hanover. I don't think we'll manage it in one day. Not at his age.'

She let out a snort of despair, her left eye still moist.

'Then we'll stop somewhere for the night,' I said, and Martha asked where the hell we were supposed to stop, we couldn't exactly spend the night at a motorway service station or in Nuremberg or Würzburg. She'd checked out the route, she said, and when you check out a route like that looking for somewhere to spend someone's last night, you quickly realise there's not a single place in the entire country that's suitable for a last night. Germany is too drab for last nights.

Martha slammed the palm of her hand on the bar, upon which the barman looked up and suggested Lake Constance.

'Lindau,' he said. That's where he was from, he said, and he wouldn't hear a bad word about Lake Constance. 'Go to Lindau.'

When you're stumped for ideas yourself, you might as well do what others tell you to. Sometimes it's best to just drift.

'Okay,' we said. 'Lindau.' Then we stared into our glasses and thought about our own last nights.

'I just want to die in bed,' Martha said. 'The main thing is not to be alone. A view would be nice. I mean, I'd rather not be in a hotel room in New York with a window looking out on an air shaft. A bed with a view of the sea in a place with no memories. I don't want to die somewhere I was once young. No coming full circle, like you've been reduced to a repetition of yourself. A Greek island, maybe. Yeah, I could imagine that.'

'I'd like to veer off a coastal road,' I said. 'A Greek island would work for me too. I just don't want to have enough time to think back over everything. I don't want to have to think and die at the same time.'

Right, Let's Go

Drawn curtains, washed dishes, four packed cardboard boxes and an empty wardrobe. The flat was ready to be left. Kurt stood in the hall, holding himself upright in his daughter's arms.

When Martha was born, this grim council block was brand new. Back then, young families were moving in. Now, the parents who remained were dying here. Most of their kids had escaped, some of them by studying, going abroad for a while and moving to Berlin like Martha, I imagine. I'd never been here before, yet it all felt familiar. I grew up on a main road in Hamburg, in a building just like this one, in a flat in which I hated every object. We'd never talked about it, only mentioning our childhoods in anecdotes we were unable to laugh at. It was as if we'd just fallen out of the sky one day – or been chucked out, more like. Martha and I were twenty when we first met, by which point we'd already severed ourselves from our backgrounds, not cleanly but systematically, and so I only understood now, in this flat, in these three poky rooms with nicotine-brown walls, that this past was what wordlessly bound us together.

Kurt's luggage comprised a pink kids' suitcase, a Lidl shopping bag and an aluminium crutch. Everything else was to stay here, and Martha would have to clear out the flat later. He'd asked her to.

It would be the only thing left to do. Clear out his stuff, pick up every item, stow the memories, pack them into boxes, cry over photos, over postcards she'd sent him, never guessing how much they meant to him. Clear it all out. Blot it all out.

He'd never said much. We were the daughters of fathers who'd only found time to talk to us after they'd retired. We explained the internet to them and they explained the weather. Their love came so late that we barely knew what to do with it. We just accepted it with gratitude. But we had little to give, and nothing at all to give back.

'Have a seat,' Kurt said. He'd made coffee even though his stomach couldn't take it any more. It was so bitter ours couldn't take it either, but we didn't tell him that.

Above the oak sideboard was a yellowish rectangle. Another pale square adorned the wall to the right of the TV. The pictures weren't gone long; compared to the rest of the walls, the patches they had left were practically white. Anything that could possibly have generated money was gone. The line between minimalism and poverty is thin but unmistakable. Nothing in here had ever been stylish. The kitchen was bare save for a few empties waiting to be brought to the bottle bank.

We sat on threadbare cushions on the kind of three-piece suite that used to be an essential part of every marriage, which he was no doubt still paying off long after his wife left him. All that remained at the end of a marriage was the sofa, upon which you could either get drunk or shoot yourself.

'How nice that you're coming along,' Kurt said to me. 'Lucky me, eh, being chauffeured around by two knockouts like yourselves?'

All three of us started nodding and I feared we'd never stop. Nodding because we didn't know what else to say. All the things I'd nodded to in my life, like the reincarnation of some nodding bloody dog. I'm the kind of person who sits on a kitchen chair nodding while she's being walked out on. And I would be sitting like that behind the wheel for the next eight hours. I would stare at the lane ahead, nodding and clenching my teeth. I should have brought my bite splint, I thought.

Kurt looked around the living room, stroking his armrest. There were no pets here, no plants either, and his pent-up affection had to be released somewhere.

'Right,' Kurt said. 'Shall we go then?'

Martha was the first to jump up, with an impatience I'd never witnessed before. Maybe she was hoping something would change if she just steamed through these last few hours.

I carried his little pink suitcase down the two flights of stairs and waited outside on a street with speed bumps, opposite a playground with swings dangling from rusty chains. The children had run away long ago. How do you say goodbye to a neighbourhood that's already dead?

I could hear Kurt talking to a neighbour on the stairs, saying something about a holiday in Switzerland with his daughter. Yes, it would be lovely, absolutely. Who's going to believe that, I wondered. Who goes on holiday to Switzerland these days when it's cheaper to fly to Spain?

The neighbour laughed loudly and obliviously, wishing Kurt a nice holiday as she closed the door.

'Right, let's go,' he said as he joined me on the street. He led the way, his crutch tapping on the tarmac. It was a sentence we'd hear many more times, of that I was sure. Whenever it's clear that no one wants to, no one has the guts to, somebody eventually has to say it: 'Right, let's go.' And then they head off to ruin their life.

Kurt led us to his car, which, as Martha had said, had been parked a street over for more than a year. It was waiting there by the kerb, lustreless, last year's blossoms plastered all over it.

'I didn't get around to washing it,' he said, handing me the key. He insisted on sitting in the back. He'd never sat in the back of his own car, he said, no one had. 'The back seat is as good as new.'

It was the only thing that was as good as new. He'd done a lot of ruminating in this car, he said; he used to come here to think. He liked to do his thinking on wheels, even if they didn't turn. Crushed beer cans lay in the footwell, the ashtray was hidden beneath a heap of butts, CDs gathered dust on the seats. Dangling helplessly from the mirror was a fir-shaped air freshener that had given up the ghost long ago.

'A 1996 Volkswagen Golf,' Kurt said. 'Twenty years accident-free. Martha will inherit the insurance, if nothing else.'

I turned the key and heard a low croak. We reanimated a corpse, wound down the windows and pulled away.

***

He'd spent his life in this city, had moved here in his mid-twenties and never left, apart from a few package holidays. I tried to imagine seeing my city for the last time. Is your final look back as full of awe as your first glimpse, albeit for different reasons? Can you believe that your greatest hopes have turned into last memories, scenes of a squandered life that will leave no trace on your city? Not one place that will remember you. If you're really unlucky, they'll start selling vegan ice cream where your favourite bar used to be, a townhouse with floor-to-ceiling windows will get built where your bookshop once was, and the block where you had your first flat-share will be torn down to make room for an Aldi.

'It's funny, you know,' Kurt said. 'I never really liked Hanover. Such an ugly city.'

'You never wanted to leave,' Martha said. 'You always said this is home, this is where your friends are.'

'Bah, friends. Friends just abandon you in the end. For women, children, work, because of booze, because of illness, there's always something more important. Friends, my arse.'

He nodded, and we shook our heads in vehement disagreement. Martha started talking about emergencies, about how friends are there for you when you really need them.

'In an emergency,' Kurt said, 'it's not friends you need. In an emergency you need a good doctor or lawyer. You need friends for the good times. The bad times you can handle on your own. It's when you're happy you need friends. Who wants to celebrate alone? Happiness can be shared, but not sorrow. Sorrow just ends up being doubled.'

On this point he was absolutely right, and never more so than right then. I put the car into fourth gear and thought about all the chilled bottles of prosecco I'd drunk on my own over the past few years. 'To me!' I'd say as I got blind drunk.

The city thinned out ahead of us, just its dregs lining the last stretch of road before the autobahn. Council flats, brothels, a car testing centre, discounters, outlets, one last McDonald's. The motorists of Hanover drove like they were possessed. In the back, Kurt started coughing and rattling. 'My God!' Martha said when she turned around, as he feebly attempted to wave away her horror. She handed him a tissue and when she got it back, it was flecked with blood.

'Pull over somewhere, Betty!' she said.

I swerved at full speed into an exit to a service station, where she handed Kurt a bottle of water and wiped the blood from his chin.

When he was able to speak again, he said, 'Bloody hell, Betty, the way you drive, I could've saved myself the money for the clinic.'

He leaned back with what appeared to be a smile.

'You know what I haven't eaten in ages? A petrol station hot dog. With a nice big blob of mustard.'

He asked Martha if he could have one, if she'd get him one, just a sausage, no roll, and as she was getting out, she turned to me and asked, 'Want one too?'

I nodded. A sudden fear gripped me that we wouldn't make it to Switzerland, that we wouldn't arrive safely. In this context, the word 'safe' was absurd, of course. But I didn't want him slipping away in the back seat. I didn't know the first thing about dying.

'Do you smoke, Betty?' he asked from the back.

Rarely had I craved a cigarette as much as I did right then. Kurt handed me one of his roll-ups, and I gave him a light. After a couple of drags, his cough subsided, and the only sounds he made were of pure pleasure.

'So Martha tells me you live on your own.'

'Yes,' I said. 'I'm pretty used to it by now.'

'Don't get too used to it. It'll drive you round the bend, Betty. People who live alone think too much, round and round in circles they go. It makes you dizzy, so dizzy you think you're going to throw up. Believe me, I know what I'm talking about.'

Martha was standing in front of the car, holding three hot dogs and screaming at the windscreen. Her rage was directed solely at me.

'What the hell is wrong with you?' she yelled.

I stubbed out my cigarette and opened the passenger door. In the rear-view mirror, I saw Kurt wink at me.

'Jesus Christ!' Martha slid into her seat and thrust a hot dog into my hand. 'Why don't you spit a bit of blood onto it too while you're at it, for the flavour? Honestly, you're unbelievable.'

'Calm down, sweetheart. I've always enjoyed smoking with women. Cigarettes and women, now that's my idea of heaven.'

'Your idea of heaven?' Martha snorted. 'If it wasn't for your idea of heaven, we wouldn't be sitting here now.'

'You wouldn't be sitting here now, that's for sure. Your mother was a magnificent smoker. If she hadn't been so good at smoking, she wouldn't have caught my eye. I don't know how she did it, but she used to send the smoke rings floating up out of the corner of her mouth. There was always a halo hovering above her. I know it's hard to imagine it now, but your mother smoked her way to sainthood. I soon found out she was anything but a saint, but when I first met her, let me tell you, she was a Madonna!'

Kurt looked at the sausage in his hand, examining it with a fascination that's probably only possible to muster either very early or very late in life. Maybe some kind of affection for the world finally takes hold of you right before the end. As he bit into the sausage, he emitted a low hum of satisfaction.

***

34

'Maybe we shouldn't stop for the night after all,' Martha whispered after checking Kurt was asleep behind us. 'Something feels off. There's something up with him.'

'Hardly surprising under the circumstances, is it?'

'No, something else. I don't know what.'

We listened to his breathing. It was fitful, with long pauses between gulps of air.

'The appointment is tomorrow at two,' I said. 'And tomorrow is tomorrow, even if we get there today.'

'Fucking physics.'

Martha pressed her uneasiness back into the seat. It was all too cramped for her. She exhaled slowly, like she was trying to create some space for herself on the inside.

'I think I need a fag,' she said.

I instinctively slowed down, as if I, of all people, was about to give her a lecture on the evils of smoking.

'What?' She wasn't whispering any more. 'This is an ashtray on wheels, what do you want me to do?'

'In the back, in my jacket pocket.'

She reached behind her and lingered there for quite a while, then grabbed my jacket and asked whether I noticed a funny smell. I sniffed but smelled nothing. Just the odour of the three of us. Tension, sadness, fear, age. And not enough space. It smelled like a cage. That's when it occurred to me. The distinctive cage smell that always emanates from the same source: urine.

'Should I stop?' I asked.

'No, let him sleep.'

She lit cigarettes for us both and said, 'Tell me about your mess of a life so I can forget about mine for a while.'

I ran my thumbs up and down the steering wheel and sighed.

'I live the kind of life,' I said, 'that generations of women before us fought for. You can't call that a mess. I am the embodiment of maximum freedom.'

'Exactly. You're getting peculiar. It's about time you fell in love again.'

'I beg your pardon, how am I getting peculiar?!'

'You're cantankerous. That's putting it mildly. To be quite honest, you're turning into a cynic.' Martha looked at me.

'Right. And falling in love is the solution?'

For years now, people had been advising me to fall in love. Like that would save me, like I needed to be saved. Like I didn't have better things to do.

'What happened to the last guy?' she continued.

'Who?'

'The artist or whatever he was.'

'He had tattoos.'

'So? You can't feel tattoos.'

'I'm done with tattooed men,' I said. 'They never stop talking. Worse than anglers they are. His explanations of his forearms were interminable. His life story in ink. Family on the right, friends on the left. Genealogical tree, twists of fate. When I first started having sex, men would use their scars to tell me their life stories. It didn't take long. The appendectomy, the skating accident, the torn meniscus. No one had more scars than that. Now there are the bypasses too, but they're quick to tell. A heart attack is unsentimental. Tattoos, though, are stories seared into flesh. I'll tell you what, this generation is well prepared for dementia. When they have trouble remembering something, they'll just have to look at their bodies, everything else will be stored in the cloud. They should go ahead and tattoo their password onto their wrists right now.'

'Jesus, sorry I asked.'

Martha wound down the window to let out the smoke, the bad atmosphere, the stink of urine.

'I don't want to talk about it,' I said. 'About men.'

'Fine. Me neither. It's boring, anyway.'

'You start at ten years of age, constantly obsessing about boys. Constantly miserable. It's so seamless. You spend three or four decades droning on about men, then you start droning on about your ailments. What a waste of a life.'

'You forgot the kids in between.'

'You can say that again.'

'Shh, be quiet for a minute.' Martha was whispering again. We tilted our heads, as if that would help us hear better.

'Is he still breathing?'

'I think so,' I said, slowing down.

Kurt was breathing like a fish. Every few seconds his mouth popped open, as if he was blowing little bubbles.

'Maybe he's in a deep sleep,' I said.

'Why is he doing this to me?' Martha glared ahead at the road, not expecting an answer, not even from herself.

I put my foot down on the accelerator – I just wanted to get to where it would all be over – while Martha searched for a radio station she couldn't find. Just snatches and static, as though we were driving through a no man's land far removed from any frequency. We had an elephant in the car we couldn't talk about, so we were silent, but it wasn't a comfortable silence. Dying is torture, it should be abolished. There should just be life and death, with nothing in between. A sense of release washed over me when I heard a groan from the back seat. In the mirror, I could see Kurt trying to orient himself. No sign of Switzerland, just the A7 somewhere between Fulda and Würzburg. I was doing my best, but Germany is a long country.

Kurt leaned forwards and asked if we could hear a noise.

'What noise?' I said. 'I don't hear anything.'

'A kind of clicking, very low … There. Can you hear it?'

'He's right,' Martha said.

'There it is again! Hear it, Betty?'

It was an intermittent, even scraping sound.

'What is it?' I asked.

Kurt smiled. 'He's thirsty.'

I squinted as I tried to make out the needle. These days I could only see distant objects clearly. Up close, things were disappearing, vanishing a little more every month.

'The tank's half-full,' I said.

'It's the oil. You can't see it, you just hear it. He needs oil. And while we're at it,' he said, 'I need a beer.'

'You must think we came down with the last shower! We've only been on the road four hours.'

He's drinking himself away, Martha once said to me. He's dissolving himself. In a drinker, everything liquefies. Head, heart, and finally the body. Everything melts away, is no longer solid. She'd been referring not just to her father, but to our friend Jon too. Back when Jon was still alive, just about, and none of us was managing to haul him back to sobriety. You stand there with your arms empty, Martha had said, hugging someone who disappeared long ago.

Now she sat in silence, biting her lips raw.

'But it's true,' Kurt said. 'We've always boozed together.' He gave a dry, slightly bloody laugh. 'He's a fast drinker, I'm afraid. Better get a five-litre bottle.'

'Five litres?' I asked.

'Or ten?' He looked lost there in the back seat. 'I don't know,' he said. 'We haven't been out on the road in a long time, and then there's the mountains. We've never been in the mountains. Just imagine, my whole life I've only ever driven across flat land. A very northern German life, when you think about it.'

I exited at the next service area and Kurt crawled out of the car, his crutch tapping ahead of him.

'I'll go get us something to drink.' He wore the expression of someone who would have to force his way through dancing mobs to get to the bar, when in fact there were just two other cars parked here. A girl was sitting alone in the passenger seat of one, crying. Her right eye was swollen and would soon turn black.

This innocent Wednesday in April, wanting nothing to do with all the misery, silently darkened. I'd given up on religion in my teens, yet whenever the sky clouded over and the rain refused to fall, I still often thought: God has shut the window, and we've been left all alone.

The girl sat there defenceless, staring out of a black limousine with a six-figure price tag. There was something familiar about her, but whether it was from a film or the past, I couldn't say. Perhaps it was just the look in her eyes I'd seen before, a look that suggested she'd given up hope of being rescued long ago. She couldn't have been more than fourteen.

I opened the bonnet of the Golf, pulled out the dipstick, wiped it down, checked the oil level.

'Well?' Martha asked. 'Is he right, or is he just looking for an excuse to get pissed?'

'The engine's drying up,' I said. 'You'd better go in and help him.'

'I'm not carrying his sodding beer for him.'

'Carry the oil, then.'

'He trained his car well, didn't he? "We've always boozed together." What a load of crap, that "We're old pals" bullshit. It's a fucking car! No one's best friend should be a car.'

'Certainly not a Golf, anyway.'

'I mean, doesn't he want to experience something beautiful, say something meaningful? There must be one thing he'd like to do. Last things, champagne, oysters, the sea, a mountaintop. Anything but a beer from a petrol station. Under a grey sky at the arse end of Germany.'

There were tears in Martha's left eye, and this enraged her even more.

'The man is a dead loss! "I'm content, honey bunny, I have everything I need." Right. A TV, a reclining armchair and a beer in the fridge. "Content, honey bunny." God, it makes me sick!'

Kurt shouted over at us from the petrol station shop. He was calling Martha's name. It looked like he'd been standing there for a while.

39

'Better take his bag with you,' I said, and she nodded, took the bag of nappies from the back seat and walked over to him with a forced smile. I watched them disappear into the shop together, her hand hovering at his back without touching it.

As I peered into the engine compartment, I found myself hoping he wouldn't make it, that he'd snuff it after the next bend. I wished for a head-on collision to end our journey. I was wishing I knew enough about cars to meddle with this one, I was fantasising about a seized piston, when a car door opened beside me and closed again with a muffled thud. The more expensive the car, the quieter it is. If you're rich enough, you can have your peace.

He was a wiry guy. With one hand, he grabbed the girl's hair, as if he was trying to rip out clumps of it, and with the other, he shoved a bar of Kinder chocolate between her lips and started the engine. All the while, she stared square ahead. Silently, the car glided past me and out on to the A7, leaving in its wake a squalid sense of my own spinelessness.

'We should've taken the girl with us,' I said to Martha as she handed me a litre of oil.

'She was a child.'

'Exactly.'

'You can't just take other people's kids. No matter how much you'd like to. It's against the law.'

'It would be a small crime to end a big one.'

'That's how every war begins.'

'In here!' Kurt said behind me. He knocked on the oil tank with his crutch.

'You can't smoke here,' Martha said. 'This is a petrol station.'

'Bah, what a load of cobblers. In the old days, the petrol attendants used to have lit fags hanging out of their mouths all day. Anyway, if they do see me, what are they going to do about it?'

He leaned against the Golf with his beer and cigarette. He was right: the world could go fuck itself.

I poured in a litre, checked it again, poured in a second litre and then a third. The car was a bottomless pit. When we finally made it back out on the road, I savoured the sound of the lubricated engine.

'Sure you don't want one?' Kurt asked us. 'I bought a couple extra beers just in case.'

'Not while I'm driving,' I said, and Martha pointed out it was her who'd bought the beers. Kurt's bank account was already closed.

'But I've no debts,' he said. 'You won't be left with a cent of debt. You'll break even. And you can hold on to the car, of course. And I still have the stereo, the Kenwood.'

'Great, a CD player with a tape deck,' Martha said.

'It's top of the range!'

'Nobody uses those things any more.'

'That's not my fault. Collectors might be interested in it.'

'Maybe. I don't want to talk about it,' she said. 'I don't want any of this. I mean, what the hell is going on? Smoking, drinking, Switzerland, dying?'

Kurt swiped the air with his hand, swatting away her questions like flies.

'If it weren't for women,' he said out of nowhere, 'I'd be a rich man. They fleeced me, the lot of them. Take your mother. She gave me a camera when we got married, and then when we got divorced she demanded it back. Unbelievable.'

Kurt shook his head for emphasis. We kept our mouths shut.

'That's women for you,' he continued. 'Fall in love with them, and they'll clean you out. Not you Martha, obviously. In your case, Betty, I'm not so sure.'

'This must be the hundredth time I've heard that story,' Martha said. 'It's more than thirty years ago now. I've been listening to the same stories from the both of you for more than thirty years, and never, not once, have you said anything nice about each other. It's a miracle I got married myself.'

41

'A miracle, or plain stupidity,' Kurt said.

In truth, it had been neither. Martha and Henning had decided to get married so that their health insurance would cover their IVF. Only for married couples, only for women under forty. And now Martha was running out of time. If she didn't get pregnant within the next six months, they would end up either childless or destitute. Possibly both.

'Cut it out, Kurt!' Martha had turned around to face him and was pulling at her seatbelt, but it just tightened with every tug.

'All I'm saying is you need to watch out, young lady. Women can be cleaned out by their husbands these days. You might end up paying him maintenance so he can keep painting his funny little pictures.'

'They're not pictures, they're animations.'

'And you can thank women like your mother for it!'

Kurt had talked himself into a rage. 'Emancipation. Self-actualisation. What a load of bollocks! Your mother actualised herself so well she forgot there are other people in the world. And what does she do in the end? She goes off and marries a bald, rich fool! Oh well, at least it meant I didn't have to pay maintenance any more, I suppose.'

I concentrated on driving faster and faster. Kurt wasn't a bad man, he just hadn't moved with the times. He'd been steamrolled by them, and no one had warned him.

'And who funded them, all those bra burners, who paid for their dungarees? The ex-husbands! And then off they went to France in their brand-new Volkswagen Beetles, the pill stuffed into their glove compartments. The kids shunted off to granny. And when the money was gone, they couldn't get remarried fast enough, to pansies with degrees.'

I stamped on the accelerator, feeling fury in my right foot and something like understanding in my left. I wasn't moving with the times either, a realisation that had dawned on me shortly after my fortieth birthday and hardened each time I watched the parties going on beneath my window.

Martha's breathing was short, hard and loud. The pressure had built up inside her and was now desperately looking for a valve. She grabbed a cigarette and proceeded to smoke it in the aggravated, hissing way only a non-smoker can.

'I'll throw you out of the car, Kurt, if you're not careful,' she said, and he pointed out that it was still *his* car, at least for today.

***

The hotel had looked luxurious on the internet. Now, though, we were standing in a small, dark lobby, the bar was closed, the pool dirty, the rooms not ready yet. Kurt disappeared off to the toilet as soon as we arrived. The façade was being renovated, the receptionist informed us. Which meant a view of scaffolding instead of Lake Constance, and builders gawping in at Kurt when he opened his eyes for the very last time.

Martha tried to explain to the young man that her father would be spending his last – literally last – night here, a night that was probably as important as one's wedding night, maybe even more so. Had the receptionist ever thought about that? Could he imagine it? Had he ever given a moment's thought to anything in his entire life?

The man looked over at me, obviously hoping I'd intervene. I just nodded, but whether it was in solidarity with Martha or the receptionist, I wasn't quite sure. Unfortunately, the hotel wasn't equipped for severely depressed guests, he explained, especially during the off-season. He could have a bottle of prosecco brought to the room, plus flowers if we wanted, and the peanuts were on the house too, but the hotel lacked the resources, not to mention the two additional stars, necessary for a last night, he said, offering to cancel our reservation and book us into the Grand Hotel on the other side of the lake.

'I'm not going to take up residence in the Grand Hotel on my last day,' Kurt growled, having struggled back from the toilet with astonishing speed. 'Is there a TV here?' he asked. 'Maischberger will be on in a minute. I never miss her. She's a smart cookie, that lady.'

Same old routine, anything to avoid hassle. Martha bit her tongue. Kurt looked at her.

'This is what I want,' he said. 'I'm not going to start a new life now, am I?'

His smile seemed to be apologising for a life in which everything had simply happened to him, a life he had fallen into.

We checked into two rooms, asked for a restaurant recommendation, dragged Kurt there and ordered roast pork, of which he only managed to eat half. Above his head hung an iced gingerbread heart. *Every cloud has a silver lining*, it said.

I ordered another half-litre of Riesling and we gazed out the window at a lit-up statue of a lion, the glassy surface of Lake Constance, boats with names like *Konstanz* and *Lindau*. Nothing disturbed the idyll, apart from us.

'It's pretty here,' Kurt said. 'Reminds me of Lake Maggiore. Ever been?'

'No,' I said when Martha didn't respond.

'It's where Hemingway recovered from his war injuries,' Kurt said. 'In Stresa. Do you know Hemingway? He was a real tough guy. Wrote standing up.'

'Because of his back problems,' Martha said.

'No,' I said. 'Because of his piles.'

'He had piles?'

'Yeah, first the war, then Cuba, all that spicy food. The poor bastard could barely sit down.'

'Christ, Betty, you hate every writer who's not you, don't you? Even the dead ones!'

'Do you write too, Betty?'

'Yes. Lying down.'

'Interesting. I'd never have guessed – you're too good-looking to be a writer.'

'Well, she hardly ever writes anything,' Martha interjected.

'And you manage to make a living?'

'No,' I said. 'I've been dead for three years.'

Martha kicked me under the table, but Kurt laughed. 'The dead,' he said, 'they're great people. Very laid-back, all the dead folk I've met so far.'

He took another slug and leaned back. 'Yes,' he said. 'Lake Maggiore. I'd love to go back one day.'

'But …' Martha searched for the right words. 'I thought you wanted to die.'

'It might be nice to unwind a bit beforehand.'

'It's the morphine,' Martha whispered to me. 'He's not in his right mind.'

'When did you visit Lake Maggiore, Kurt?'

'When I was young, in my mid-twenties. With my first girlfriend, Francesca. I was a late bloomer, shy, and to make matters worse I had these milk-bottle glasses. The girls weren't exactly lining up,' he said. 'But then along came Francesca. She was half-Italian. According to her mother, anyway. She'd never met her father. She was born around the end of the war, it was all a bit of a free-for-all back then.'

'You never mentioned her before.' Martha looked scandalised.

'I had a life too, you know, before I met your mother,' he said. 'Especially in those days. I looked like a Sicilian. I still had my hair, dark curls – people thought I was in the mafia. Which wasn't an advantage, not at all, until I met Francesca. I got my driving licence especially for her and bought a car, a second-hand Opel Kadett. She wanted to go to Italy, to see everything: Genoa, Florence, Rome, all the way down to Naples. Not Venice, she said that was too romantic. We'll go there on our honeymoon, she said.'

Kurt gestured to the waiter for another beer. His eyes had the distinctive sheen that appears when alcohol mixes with nostalgia and the mood turns fragile.

'We only made it as far as Stresa. First love, first holiday, but it wasn't meant to be.'

'What happened?'

How easy it is to think you know your parents, to forget they were once young and desperate like us, except they had to stop being young and desperate a lot earlier because we arrived, though that didn't end the despair, just the being young bit. There are two things that force you to grow up: the birth of your first child and the death of your parents. Martha was on the brink of both.

'She dumped me,' Kurt said. 'In a bar. Left me for a real Italian. He looked like something out of a magazine: polo shirt, gold chain and a boat. Me and my Opel didn't stand a chance. The fella just sat down at our table and stole my girl from under my nose. And I did nothing about it, didn't try to chase him off, didn't fight for her. Off you go then, I said. The next morning she came back to our room and packed her case. Take care of yourself, Kurt love, she said, and she was gone.'

He took a large swig of beer.

'I drove on to Genoa on my own and went on a bender. Take care of yourself, my arse, I did the exact opposite, just to spite her. Genoa is a loud city, mangy. Vespas, rubbish, bars, raving lunatics. It was a cesspit back then. Whores on every corner. That's the best thing about harbour cities, the whores. And drugs everywhere.'

I knew those cities, where people live as if their ship will leave port the next morning. Port cities are the home of the last night. One last night after another, and the ship never sails.

'And you want to go back there?' Martha asked. 'To Stresa? Where you were dumped?'

'I don't know,' Kurt said. 'It's so long ago now. That's the hardest thing. You're always thinking back to when you were young. Back to when you made the wrong decisions, to when life took different turns but you weren't able to do anything about it.'

Martha and I just nodded sadly. Maybe, like me, she was re-solving to have fewer regrets at the end of her life.

It had taken him a long time to realise that you can't escape where you come from, Kurt said, that all you do is vary your parents' mistakes, that each generation just finds smarter ways to cock things up and ruin their lives. Leave as little damage behind as possible, that was the only advice he could offer. 'Don't do harm,' he said, and finished his beer.

***

Between our beds stood a pine table, on top of it a telephone that probably hadn't been used in years. We'd eaten the two rancid little chocolate hearts that had been placed on our pillows, and the minibar was empty except for three bottles of mineral water and a packet of peanuts. Martha peered into the little fridge in frustration and fantasised about pouring herself a gin and tonic. She hadn't had one in ages, she said. We must have been kids when we last thought a drink in our hands would get us through the night.

'So, are we going to Lake Maggiore?' I asked, as if that were a real option. Martha looked at me pensively.

'It was fifty years ago. I mean, fifty years, we're not talking about old times here, we're not talking about memories. It's all just projection. I've never even heard of this woman. Anyway, look at him: he's coughing up blood, pissing himself, he needs morphine. Do you really think we'd be doing him any favours?'

Weirdly, seeing as I never remember poetry, a line by Pablo Neruda popped into my head. I must have come across it in my teenage years, back when my brain could still retain some of what I read.

'"Isn't it better never than late?"' I said, and it sounded so prosaic that Martha thought the words were my own.

47

'That's the question,' she said. Having given up on finding a drink, she lay down on the bed and scratched at the woodchip on the walls instead.

'Odd, isn't it? It's the last thing I'd want to do, go back to where some bloke dumped me. On his first holiday, too. It's pure masochism. Now I know where I get it from. It's starting to make sense,' Martha said. She couldn't understand why things start to make sense so late – too late, in fact. 'By the time it all makes sense to you, you're dead,' she said.

'Maybe he just wants to see how miserable she is now. She's bound to be miserable if she ended up with a gold-chain-wearing boatman on Lake Maggiore.'

'That's if she's still alive,' Martha said. 'And still lives there.'

'Maybe he's looking into it now?'

'Oh, please.' She shook her head. 'He'll be fast asleep now. He drank himself to exhaustion. He won't be looking into anything. And neither will I. My purpose in life isn't to save my parents. Even if that's why they brought me into the world.'

'Does your mother know about all this?' I asked.

'About Francesca?'

'No. About you taking him to Switzerland.'

'I told her.'

'And?'

'Typical, she said. He blagged his way through life, she said, and now he can't even die like a man. Can you believe that? "Die like a man." Why do men have to die like men, why can't they just be allowed to die like everyone else? Or not die, like whatever.'

'Did they ever love each other, do you think?'

'They might have needed each other. I don't know. I don't want to know any more.'

We heard the toilet flush in the next room. In every hotel I'd ever stayed in, the walls were so thin that I felt I was being watched, even while I slept. You're never alone, just lonely.

'You don't happen to have some weed, do you?' Martha asked.
'No,' I said. 'I haven't smoked in years. I wouldn't even know where to buy weed now.'

'There's always the park,' she said, as if she were a regular there.

'The last time I walked through Görlitzer Park, they didn't even offer me anything. You feel really old when the dealers stop hassling you.'

But Martha said she'd heard it would come full circle eventually.

'When we're sixty,' she said, 'we'll be back on their radar again.'

'It's absurd, though, isn't it? We stop taking drugs at the age we need them most.' As I spoke, I realised I'd forgotten to take my tablet that morning. There were still drugs, just different ones. I went into the bathroom and swallowed a citalopram.

I hadn't told Martha I was still taking them. It was she who'd peeled me from my bed and brought me to the doctor one morning almost two years ago. I was only capable of nodding by that stage; I hadn't used my voice in so long I could barely talk. The way you look right now, you won't need to say anything, she'd said, dragging me out the door, where the sun pointed a finger at me, dumping the spring at my feet. As if I had any use for it.

It's not that bad, I'd said to the doctor. But I couldn't explain why I was sitting there in front of him, why someone had had to escort me there. How could I sit in front of a doctor without an appointment and say: It doesn't hurt at all? He watched me drooping in the chair like an eighty-year-old, unable to hold myself upright even when sitting down.

How long haven't you been able to sleep, how long haven't you been able to concentrate, work? Get out of bed? Do you shower? Do you buy groceries? Do you eat? Do you think about killing yourself? Do you think about killing someone else? Question after question. I didn't know how long it had been going on. Six, seven months maybe. Not long, I said, no, it would pass, I was sure. Everything passes eventually, doesn't it?

Rock-solid, he'd said, a rock-solid case of depression, and I didn't understand his phrasing, because nothing in my life was solid, rock-solid, tangible any more. He gave me a prescription and instructions on how to gradually increase the dose. Just to get you back on your feet, he said, and I took them every day, and after a week I got out of bed, after two weeks I went out, and no one seemed to have noticed I'd been gone. I picked up a new prescription every three months and never saw the doctor again. But a feeling had taken root, one I hadn't been able to shake off since, a feeling that the more I knew about myself, the less I trusted myself.

'You should stop taking those pills,' Martha said. 'You can't be popping them for the rest of your life. You haven't written a single book since you started them.'

'In fairness, I'd only written one book before I went on them.'

'High time you wrote a new one, then.'

She had some nerve getting on my case tonight. It was patently obvious that she too was running away, fleeing. We both had plenty of practice in that regard, but it was Martha who was harder to stop. Once she'd decided to run away from something, no matter how imminent and urgent it was, she was gone. When she didn't want to talk about herself, she'd interrogate everyone else until she'd squeezed the last drop of information out of them. Her tenacity was feared. Nobody wanted to meet her when she was up to her neck in problems. You'd be left feeling like it was your life that was a catastrophe. Martha would then sit across from you in triumph, as if to say: See, sort yourself out before you start giving me advice.

'I'm afraid to,' I said. 'I don't want it to start again.'

'The writing?'

'The sadness.'

'Maybe they're related.'

'Of course they are. Everything's related, that's the problem.'

'How do others manage?'

'What others?'

'Other writers. You do know other writers, don't you?'

I knew very few people who weren't writers, something Martha liked to tease me about. 'You need to meet normal people again,' she'd say. And I'd go to the gym, the tax office, the multiplex, the department store and the pub on the corner, spending days and nights there, at the end of which I'd stagger home, resolving to keep away from these normal people for a while. They're all weirdos – that's why you can write whole books about them. When you run out of ideas, all you have to do is go to your local and start recording. I'd spent half my life with so-called normal people and was glad to be rid of them. My upbringing was a foul-smelling affair, it reeked from my pores, and the stench was regularly mistaken for coolness. But people who've spent their youth in the nastiest dives in St Pauli because they couldn't stick it at home aren't cool, they're just damaged.

Martha knew this, even though I only met her after all that. I met everyone after. I'd made such a decisive break with my past that I wasn't even able to mine it for material, for all that people kept advising me to do so. I'd have to find something to mine, though, and soon.

'The others are on cocaine and gin, Ritalin now too,' I said. 'Apparently you can write twenty pages in one sitting when you're on Ritalin. As long as you're not someone who actually needs Ritalin.'

'Hmm.'

'Some people work. Sober, I mean. They write in the mornings. Every morning while the kids are at school. It shows in their books.'

'How do you mean?'

'They're nice and tidy. The kind of books everyone likes.'

'Nothing wrong with that.'

'No, but it's pointless. For me, anyway. What are you supposed to write when bombs are exploding every day, when guys are blowing themselves up, speeding down promenades and mowing people down who were just trying to be happy? When kids are getting on trains wielding axes and marching into shopping centres with Glocks? When tanks are rolling into cities where friends of yours live? What are you supposed to write when you realise you don't understand the world any more – I mean in an absolutely fundamental way – when all your certainties collapse, when you realise that the bubble you live in is just that, a bubble that could burst any minute?'

I couldn't stop; she'd caught me on the wrong foot. One of my wrong feet, that is. I had more than two. Who can stand on just two feet these days?

'What are you supposed to write when everything you know seems banal now, when you sense that this misery is just the beginning, that something you can't even imagine is coming. When you realise you don't have any survival skills, you wouldn't even be able to tend to the wounded, you can't get anywhere without your sat nav. You can't fly a plane, can't fire an assault rifle, you faint at the sight of blood. In your weaker moments you tell yourself that love will save the day. What are you supposed to say when everything you think you know is actually other people's knowledge, and that they don't understand anything either? When you watch the news and the reporter is talking about a chaotic situation, about conflicting reports; flags, tanks, screaming, helicopters, police cars in the background, and the earpiece slips out of her sweaty ear, and the picture wobbles, not because the picture is wobbly, but because the cameraman's legs have gone from under him, and the news anchor chats live with a president who has gone into hiding, and you pour yourself more wine because you can't get your head around any of it? What are you supposed to write? Writing takes time, it takes distance and understanding and research, but none of that's in your contract, no one's going to pay you for it, the time you need to figure out what the hell is going on.'

Martha had fallen completely silent in the other bed, but I still wasn't finished. I took a deep breath and continued. 'So you volunteer with refugees or adopt a glamorous new persona and lose yourself online. If all else fails, you can withdraw into seclusion. First you need to find that seclusion, though, but of course people are breeding like rabbits right now, as they always do when things go to shit, so that they have something to hold on to, a reason to keep going, to hang in there, and it's good to have something that's more important than anything else, and if that something happens to be a human being, even better. Not everyone has that, and it's rarely their fault. Hardly anything is our fault any more, instead it's our circumstances, our genes. You know what? I envy your father a bit,' I said in conclusion. 'It's a good time to be old enough to die.'

'Betty.' Martha turned around to face me. 'Are you sure those tablets are helping?'

'Very funny,' I said. 'The question is, how bad would I be without them?'

For a moment, I'd forgotten that she and Henning wanted a child, that Martha had been pumping herself full of hormones for eighteen months now, that she'd had three miscarriages and was about to try again. I kept forgetting because she didn't talk about it any more. Neither of us talked any more about the powerlessness and unhappiness that hounded us every day and were slowly eating away at us.

'What are we going to do if he really does want to go to Stresa?'

Martha's hands were clasped on top of the duvet. It felt like we were sharing a room in a Catholic boarding school. She looked up at the ceiling, her body so taut and straight in the bed that her tension was visible even in the dark.

'I'm the driver,' I said. 'I'll drive you wherever.'

'Wouldn't that be nice?' she said. 'Just driving around, a few more days, weeks, months. Just being on the road together, nothing lurking at the end. Nothing but a glass of wine, a view of a valley, a bit of a chat, a bit of silence. That would be enough for me.'

'Yeah, that would be nice.'

'Yeah.'

'Martha?'

'Yes.'

'What's going to happen tomorrow?'

'We're driving to Switzerland.'

'You know what I mean.'

'It's an apartment, I think,' she said. 'With staff, a doctor. Kurt will lie down on a bed, we'll say our goodbyes, and I'll go wait outside the door while they dissolve 15 milligrams of this powder, pentobarbital sodium, in water. Apparently it tastes awful. In a few minutes he'll fall into a coma, in a quarter of an hour he'll stop breathing. Then it's over, and we'll drive back to Berlin. The funeral will be Friday week. He wants to be cremated and anonymously interred. That's the plan.'

Martha tossed in her bed.

'God, I'd love a schnapps right now,' she said. 'Roast pork of all things, as if things weren't hard enough to digest already.'

'I've got some Rennie with me.'

'Course you do. Is your stomach depressed too?'

I could feel her looking over at me in the dark.

'It's so strange,' she said. 'The only thing he's ever really planned in his whole life is his death. Everything else just kind of happened to him, or rather didn't happen. It's like he really didn't want more.'

'The things we want most are often the things we need least,' I said.

'I don't think he dared want more. He wasn't brought up to want more. He's not brave, not strong, just tough. But what do

I know? All I really know about him is what he's told me. Is it normal for your own parents to be strangers?'

I didn't know. All I knew was that was the case for us and most other people I knew. But while you can have a relatively positive relationship with a stranger, some of our friends had only contempt for their parents, a feeling that had emerged when they were teenagers and hardened since. We'd never tried to understand our parents the way we did our friends. And when our parents tried to be our friends, we understood them even less. Things would improve. I wanted to believe that with every generation, things would improve, even if I myself wasn't helping to improve anything.

Martha and I barely slept that night. We listened to each other breathing, listened to the doubt and the fear and couldn't talk about it any more.

***

'Right, let's go.'

Kurt was sitting in the lobby, ready to go, when we came down. Showered, packed, breakfasted. He looked better than the day before – rested, even. It was nearly over, just a few more hours, and I could well imagine the prospect might have a soothing effect.

'Got your passports?' he asked.

'It's Switzerland. We don't need passports.'

'Not yet,' he said. 'But who knows when they might suddenly decide to seal the borders behind us? You don't want them stopping you from coming back.'

'We always find our way back. Don't worry, Kurt,' Martha said, and carried her case to the car.

We resumed our positions in the car as if we'd been on the road together for weeks. Kurt wound down the window and I started the engine, raising my eyebrows at Martha, who just raised her eyebrows back at me.

55

'How about a coffee?' I asked her. 'I need coffee. I don't care about breakfast, but without coffee …'

'Petrol station,' Martha said.

Now was not the time for my own needs. I had a tendency to get confused and think that if I was okay, everyone else would be fine too.

'In fifty metres, turn left,' a voice said. Martha enlarged the map on her phone and shrugged.

We turned into a pedestrianised street and proceeded to drive past café terraces, craft shops displaying their wares outside, clothes rails with all-weather jackets and thirty per cent reductions. We veered around a market stall selling fruit, vegetables and homemade jam. People commonly referred to in such situations as 'innocent bystanders' ducked back against the buildings, shouting abuse or else staring in disbelief. They seemed to have had plenty of practice at both. My hands were damp on the wheel.

After ten minutes and three hundred metres of pedestrianised street, we reached the main road, where a sign pointed towards the autobahn.

'Well, that was the quickest route, I suppose,' Martha said.

At the next petrol station she bought me a coffee from the machine. I had a KitKat and two cigarettes for breakfast while Kurt knocked back eight different pills in one go and launched into a monologue: Clinging to a life that had long stopped having anything to offer, it bordered on idiocy, he said. And all that stuff about the small pleasures, that was just used to flog self-help books and keep people going to church. Humbug, he called it. When he saw a kid laughing in the sunshine, he wanted to cry. Poor sod, it's all ahead of him, he would think. Apart from smoking, nothing brought Kurt pleasure any more. He was going to spend his last few euros on a pack of cigarillos, he said. It had been ten years since he'd last splashed out on cigarillos.

He shuffled over to Martha, who was at the checkout buying a motorway toll sticker, and gaped in disbelief at the price list on the wall.

'How much?' he roared. 'Thirty-five euros?'

'But then it's valid for a whole year,' the man behind the till said.

'You're having a laugh,' Kurt said. 'Drive to Switzerland to die and we get a sticker for a year. Martha, you and Betty should make a business out of it, now you've got the sticker. Typical Swiss,' he muttered, hobbling out while Martha paid.

***

Lake Constance shimmered in the rear-view mirror, it literally shimmered, and I felt sad, as I always did whenever I caught a last glimpse of something beautiful in the mirror. I'd always found it hard to leave something beautiful. Not as hard as being left, of course, but who's ever been left by a place?

The road climbed higher and higher. There were now just three hours between us and our destination. It felt as if time were skidding down the sides of the mountains. We didn't talk and didn't listen to music, because no one knew what music we ought to listen to, and because moments like these have to be borne in silence. The blacklist of music I could no longer listen to because the memories were too painful was already long enough. Even the engine struggled on quietly, suffering but not complaining.

We drove through a series of ever-longer tunnels, and after a thousand metres of darkness, a mobile phone beeped. It wasn't mine, and it wasn't Martha's either. The beeping was coming from a jacket on the back seat. Kurt fished out the phone, his hands trembling slightly.

Squinting, he read the message. He seemed to reread it several times before he said, 'Can you pull over please, Betty? I need to make a phone call.'

'It's a mobile,' Martha said. 'You can call from the car. You can call from anywhere.'

'But it's hard to hear here. And I'd like to be alone for a minute.' He looked at her beseechingly. 'I'd like to make a phone call alone and in peace.'

We had to drive through another three tunnels before the hard shoulder reappeared and we could pull over. We watched, hazard lights blinking, as Kurt paced up and down, trying to pluck up the courage to return the call. He talked to the mountains while we sat in the car. He searched for the right words, tried out one sentence after another, shook his head and looked down at the ground. Then, all of a sudden, he stood up straight.

'He's talking to someone,' Martha whispered. 'Look.'

'Yes,' I whispered back.

We observed him for a long time, so long that Martha began glancing at the clock.

'Punctuality was never one of his strengths,' she said.

'Should I honk?' I asked. 'Maybe he's forgotten us.'

Instead, Martha started waving at him and bobbing up and down in the passenger seat. Eventually she got out and took a few steps towards him, very slowly, as if approaching an animal she didn't want to scare away. Kurt glanced at her and walked off in the other direction. Meanwhile, the traffic zoomed past relentlessly. How he managed to have a conversation amid the din was a mystery to me. For a few minutes I watched the two of them standing outside, Martha staring down into the valley, Kurt at his shoes. All the standing was clearly exhausting him; he was becoming more hunched by the minute. I could see him ending the conversation, keeping hold of the phone, clutching it. Hesitantly, he turned around to face Martha and the two of them walked back to the car. In the back seat, he lit up a cigarette. His breathing was laboured; every word he uttered was like running a metre.

'How long would it take to get to Stresa?' he asked quietly. 'Is it very far?'

He looked over at me.

'No,' I said. 'About three hours.'

'She said I should call in.'

'Who did?' Martha asked, though of course we both knew.

'Francesca.' He couldn't look us in the eye. An old man as embarrassed as a boy.

'But ...' Martha was trying so hard to find the right words that in the end what made it out was the naked truth. 'But Kurt, you're dying. You've been on morphine for weeks, you can barely move, you can't control your own body, you're coughing up blood.'

'I'm well aware of that, Martha.'

I slipped out of the car, leaving the two of them alone. I wished I had someone to phone now while Kurt was having to decide between love and death, whether to put himself through the aggravation and the pain again, one final time. I wouldn't have known what to do in his shoes. Maybe I'd opt for peace, for calm, though I'd never gone for that option before. Maybe I'd tell myself that enough was enough, precisely because it had never been enough, because ultimately the hurt always outweighed the happiness. Because sometimes it's smarter to surrender than to keep fighting. Because when it's over, it's over. God knows. I could also just take three steps out on to the road and never have to make a decision again.

Martha had got out of the car too. She didn't seem any less bewildered.

'Kurt says she wants to see him. And he says she's a nurse. I don't know if that's true,' Martha said. 'But he seems to have made his mind up.'

'And she's really still living by Lake Maggiore?'

'So he says.'

'Right, let's go then.' I couldn't think of anything else to say. I was just the driver. Actually, I was Kurt's driver, or at least that had been my understanding, even if Martha took a different view.

'I just don't know,' she whispered into the roar of the passing lorries. 'I just don't know ...'

I put my arm around her and lowered my head to hear her better. In all our years together, she'd never seemed so small.

'What don't you know?' I asked.

'I mean, can we just postpone it?' She gave a helpless laugh.

'Postpone what?'

'The appointment,' she said. 'The appointment's today. I mean, can we just call up and say he doesn't feel like it today? Tell them he'd prefer to die tomorrow or next week? Will we be charged double? I mean, how does this kind of thing work?'

She began to shake, to gasp for air, and then she grew still again. The only thing Martha wanted now was for it all to stop. Everything inside her had been gearing up for this appointment, she'd braced herself, she'd had everything under control, everything up to this appointment. She'd put on a front for her sake as well as mine because it was the only way she could cope, but she couldn't keep it up any longer. She'd been strictly rationing her strength. Finding herself wanting him to die now because she herself couldn't keep going, that was too much for Martha.

'Do something,' she said. 'Anything, please.'

When a situation seems hopeless, your best option is to deal with the practicalities. I'd learned that much over the years, so I said to her in a low voice, 'Give me the number.'

While I dialled, Martha went back to the car and joined Kurt in the back seat. As they sat there with their heads leaning against each other, they made me think of a couple splitting up for 'rational' reasons and truly believing it's for the best, no matter how much it hurts. Only later, after the pain has eaten away at them so much that nothing seems temporary any more and nothing can be undone, do they realise that the decisions that hurt are rarely the right ones.

I spelled out Kurt's name and heard the tapping of fingers on a keyboard, the rustling of paper. I repeated the name, repeated the appointment, looked over at the two of them, at Kurt, who was now smoking out of the open window. Kurt, whom I'd clearly underestimated. When he caught me staring at him, he looked away. I said thank you and hung up. I stared at the Alpine panorama as I attempted to sort through the information, to clear up the confusion.

'We're going to Stresa,' I said as I got in. 'That's what Kurt wanted all along.'

'But what about Chur? The appointment? I mean, what's going on?'

A shrill note of desperation had entered Martha's voice, and I tried to explain as carefully as I could that there was no appointment, that Kurt had never made one, that they'd never even heard of him. That he – and as I said this bit, I looked at Kurt – had obviously wanted to go to Lake Maggiore from the beginning but hadn't had the guts to tell us.

Martha's desperation boiled over.

'You can't be serious!' she shouted. 'I refuse to sit in a car with this man for one more second! You drive him to that fucking lake if you want. You two can do what you like!' And with that, she got out of the car and ran off.

I let her run. She wouldn't get very far. No one gets very far on the hard shoulder. Kurt cowered in the back, a little mound of shame.

'I should've been straight with you,' he said, and I started the car and drove very slowly, hazard lights still flashing, alongside Martha.

'Yeah,' I said. 'The truth is always an option.'

'She wouldn't have taken me to see her,' he said. 'She would've refused, and I'd never have managed it on my own. The journey.' Leaning out the window, he croaked, 'You'll take me somewhere to die all right, but you won't take me somewhere to love!'

'Spare us the melodrama!' Martha barked back, and I had to agree with her.

Kurt pulled his head back in and said it was really nice that I was on his side, here, now, that he wouldn't forget it, and then he coughed up something I'd rather not have seen.

'I won't be around for much longer, that much is clear,' he said. 'And I really did plan on going to Switzerland. But then Francesca got in touch out of nowhere. After all these years. She knows about my situation. We've been emailing for months.'

'What?' Outside, Martha came to an abrupt stop and glared at her father. 'You email each other? But you can't even type!'

'I can, I'm just slow,' he said. 'With one finger.' He held his finger aloft as if to check which way the wind was blowing. 'Do you know what Francesca said to me?'

I shook my head, and Martha, who had resumed walking, was shaking her head too out on the hard shoulder.

'She said: I won't abandon you a second time.'

Kurt sighed, presumably because he thought this such a beautiful sentence, and I wondered what kind of woman this Francesca was. How desperate, lonely, sentimental she must be. But what did I know? Maybe she'd simply managed to get through life without becoming cynical, without completely ruining herself.

'Maybe she's lonely too,' Kurt said. 'Or maybe she's got some kind of helper syndrome.' He thought the latter was likely, but he didn't care.

Behind us, cars honked. We were still moving at the same pace as Martha, who was now trudging more than walking. The road sloped steeply upwards, but she persevered for another tough kilometre until we came to a tunnel and the hard shoulder ended. I opened the passenger door and she got in without a word.

'Feeling better?' I asked.

She leaned back in her seat and closed her eyes. She was afraid of tunnels, I knew that. She used to close her eyes in tunnels even when she was driving. Martha was the only woman I knew who could drive by ear. Before the accident, at least. She hadn't driven since. It wasn't fear so much as guilt, the conviction she'd done harm becoming so firmly lodged inside her that she'd turned her back not just on cars, but on people too. She'd become quieter at exactly the same speed as Jon had given up and fallen to pieces before our eyes.

But who gets through life without doing harm at some point, whether it's because of incompetence, laziness or weakness? Sometimes it's a monstrous lie, sometimes a small mistake that can't be undone. And sometimes it's sheer chance that wreaks devastation. Jon was ready for disaster years before it struck. This readiness lies within us all. Some of us spend our lives keeping it in check, that longing to give up.

Kurt opened his first beer of the day, all three of us lit up cigarettes and we got into the left-hand lane, headed for Locarno.

***

The border lay behind a bend in the road. After two hours, Switzerland was suddenly and unspectacularly over. Had it not been for the mountains, we would've got through the country in barely an hour. We didn't stop once; far too expensive to stop, according to Kurt. There was no other country he felt less inclined to spend his money in, he said. If he still had some cash and some energy, he'd drink them both away in Greece. I told him he was right. One ought to show solidarity by honouring the lost gods in the tavern of a toothless Greek.

A few men in uniform were leaning against an empty cabin at the border checkpoint. One of them was telling jokes, the others laughing dirtily as they waved through one car after another with lazy flicks of their wrists. This is where the south begins, I thought, where people stop taking themselves so seriously.

'Italy!' I heard Kurt say in the back. 'Why did I ever leave you?' This was followed by a suppressed cough.

We'd smuggled a man into the country who we knew had no intention of leaving alive, for all that Kurt kept trying to convince us otherwise. He was going to treat himself to some happiness, he'd said. A few extra days, a little holiday with no luggage and no responsibilities. Sod it, he said, that's just how I tick. Fathered by a fleeing soldier just before the end of the war, what do you expect? He leaned forwards, squeezed Martha's shoulder and nodded like a man who knew exactly what he was doing, who had everything in hand.

'Any minute now,' he said. 'Just two or three more bends in the road and Lake Maggiore will appear.'

It was barely visible under a carpet of fog. The world's most glorious scenery is never photographed in bad weather, apart from thunderstorms. A proper thunderstorm is a beautiful thing too. But fog like this was a let-down; it just blocked the view and filtered out the sun. The disappointment was etched on Kurt's face. I myself hadn't expected much of Lake Maggiore. I wasn't Hemingway, and this region's heyday was long gone.

'I wonder what she looks like now,' Kurt said. 'Old, I suppose. She's only two years younger than me, and look at me.'

Martha said that women tend to be better at taking care of themselves, that's why they live longer than men. It has nothing to do with genes, she said, they just have more love, for themselves, for the world.

'Maybe,' Kurt replied, 'But I don't fancy old women.'

Martha wound down the window. There seemed to be something musty emanating from Kurt's breath, something coming from deep inside him. I remembered hearing once that you can tell death is on its way by its stink. You can smell when someone only has a couple of days left. Not the smell of decay, that comes later. That smell I knew, I'd never forget it, but the smell of the dying is different.

'It's genetics, of course,' Kurt said.

'Love isn't a gene, for God's sake!' Martha stuck her head out the window for a quick lungful of air.

'The ability to love is hereditary. It comes from the mother,' he said. 'Or at least in my generation it did.'

'Right.'

'Nowadays you've got these men who want to do everything. Change nappies, bottle-feed. They'd breastfeed if they could. Back in the seventies, if a man walked down the street carrying a baby, the police would arrest him for kidnapping. They'd assume he was a paedophile – either that or an oddball, a hippy.'

'So men today are all hippies?'

'Hippies in suits.'

Rather than argue with him, I pointed out that we'd reached Lake Maggiore but I'd no idea where exactly in Stresa we were headed.

'Hotel Elena,' Kurt called from behind, and Martha and I bashed foreheads as we turned around to look at him. We'd both expected a private address.

'I thought you wanted to visit this Francesca woman?' Martha's voice had the grating tone it assumed whenever she was trying to brake while travelling at full speed.

'That's right,' he said. 'Francesca has a B&B called Hotel Elena.'

'Why?'

'What do you mean, why?'

I concentrated on the tight, steep twists in the road threatening to catapult us into Lake Maggiore any minute. While it was true that I dreamt of veering off a coastal road, I wanted to do it alone and by the sea.

'Why is it called a hotel if it's a B&B and Elena if her name's Francesca?'

'I don't know,' Kurt said. 'It's just a name.'

'Didn't you say she was a nurse?'

'Yeah, privately.'

'What do you mean, privately? She does it as a hobby or what?'

'It's not a hobby, she's fully trained, a qualified nurse.'

I could hear Kurt taking a deep breath, or rather attempting to take a deep breath, and the attempt ending in a coughing fit I feared would tear his lungs to shreds.

Martha was not to be distracted, however.

'Let me get this straight. This qualified nurse of yours runs a B&B for dying ex-lovers? It sounds like something out of a horror film. I'm sorry to be so blunt, Kurt, but does she realise you're completely broke? That you couldn't even pay for the trip here? That you lied to your daughter so she'd take you? Lied to her in the worst imaginable way, may I add? Treating me like I'm made of wood, like some fucking German oak that everything just bounces off, someone you feed some bullshit story about euthanasia in Switzerland just to wangle a free trip to Lake Maggiore?'

'She can't stand the sight of blood,' he said.

'Excuse me?'

'She can't stand the sight of blood. It makes her dizzy, she passes out. That's why she stopped working in the hospital.'

'That's the most ludicrous story I've heard in a long time.'

'But it's true. Her mother was a nurse, her grandmother, her great-grandmother, a dynasty of nurses. What was she to do?'

'Something else! Something that doesn't involve blood!'

'Yes, that's what she did in the end. Hotel Elena.'

I pulled into the next available parking space. We were right next to the promenade. To our left, in the fog, the lake. To our right, in the rain, a massive, ostentatious, impossibly grand hotel.

'That's where Hemingway stayed, by the way,' Kurt said.

'Swish,' I said. I hadn't realised Hemingway was filthy rich even when he was young.

'The Grand Hotel des Iles Borromées. Costs an arm and a leg to stay there.'

Still no one had told me where Hotel Elena was, nor did anyone plan on telling me, as far as I could see. Kurt and Martha were staring at the lake as if they wanted to file away this moment as their last shared memory.

I tapped the name of the hotel into my phone. A red pin appeared on the screen, just three streets away from us.

Hotel Elena was a very different class of hotel. Even the term 'B&B' seemed wide of the mark. Located right on the main square, Piazza Generale. Nothing but pizzerias and bars serving cocktails with paper parasols and glittery pom-poms. Incessant noise from the front, the stink of rubbish from the back. I was familiar with hovels like these, they were the same all over the world. It came as no surprise to me that even here, at Lake Maggiore, I'd ended up at a dump. I had a knack for winding up with the wrong people. It was the glass ceiling. I couldn't smash through. I could stand around in expensive clothes at pretentious parties but I'd always end up drinking with the bar staff. But I loved the wrong people with all my heart. Well, with what remained of it, the few proud, beautiful vestiges.

We sat in the car in front of Hotel Elena, no one daring to get out, as if another reality began beyond its confines, one that would tear us apart. A mighty whack on the roof made us jump. At first all I saw was red hair coiled in meticulous curls around a small face. The eyebrows were plucked, the lashes glued, the lips painted, the skin powdered, every image I'd had of Francesca in my head daubed in makeup. Kurt gulped audibly, and outside, she laughed, with teeth so straight and white they could only be false.

'Come on!' she called. 'There's coffee inside.'

We gave Kurt the time he needed to get out of the car first, and he needed a long, long time to arrange his limbs, his clothes and finally his hair. Eventually he got out, and they both proffered their hands like two children being forced to apologise in front of their parents. Francesca laughed even louder, a bit too loud, before putting her arms around Kurt, at which point they both fell silent.

When old people embrace, when they exchange kisses, be they shy or amorous, I feel ashamed. Not because it's embarrassing; on the contrary, I think there's something almost sacred about it. What they call 'late-life happiness' seems more real to me than young happiness, and certainly more real than middle-aged happiness, which I don't consider happiness at all but an act of neediness and boredom. In fact, I don't think there's anything quite as hackneyed and contrived as people in their forties claiming to be blissfully in love. Only when they're thirty years older am I inclined to believe them. Maybe that says more about me, maybe I think old people have the courage and hope that I gave up long ago.

Francesca's mask of makeup had shifted a centimetre, making her face look distorted. We carried the little pink suitcase through the breakfast room to the lift. She'd made up a room for Kurt on the second floor with a window looking out on the square, which was hardly likely to be a problem for the hearing-impaired, as she noted with a giggle. Beside the bed were flowers and a little bottle of grappa. On the wall, the obligatory tacky picture of the area, a watercolour of Lake Maggiore at dusk. At every halfway scenic spot in the world there are people making a living by selling their therapeutic handicrafts to dingy hotels. In my darkest moments, that seemed like an attractive career option. I would picture myself on some island, painting driftwood and otherwise just focusing on breathing in and out. Nothing would be wrong. And nothing about it would be right. Between these two poles lies the gaping void in which life unfolds.

Martha fell onto the bed and clutched the floral bedspread.

'It's awful,' she said. 'Handing him in like a dog I don't want to take along on holiday.'

'He wanted to come here, and you're not going on holiday. The parallel doesn't work at all.'

'I am handing him in, though.'

'Martha, you're doing what he asked you to.' Mind you, what he'd asked for had changed considerably over the last few hours.

'It feels like I've spent my whole life trying to please my father, and it's always left me feeling crappy,' she said. She told me about arguments that invariably ended with her caving, because it was easier, because she was afraid. She talked away her pain while talking herself deeper into her frustrated love for Kurt, only stopping when she was interrupted by a knock on the door.

Francesca came in with a strange mixture of boldness and timidity. She had a determined walk, but her hands flapped around aimlessly, picking at the flowers and curtains and, in the ultimate gesture of female awkwardness, smoothing out her skirt. She sat down on the bed beside Martha and tried to say that she'd take good care of Kurt, tried to say that it wasn't easy, meeting like this, that she wished it were under different circumstances, that Kurt could count on her, that she'd phone if he deteriorated, that she was sorry – except she didn't say any of this. The obvious was not to be spoken of. Instead, she offered us espresso and home-made cake, which Martha flatly turned down. With a little bob suggestive of a lumbago flare-up, Francesca left the room.

'Poor Francesca,' I said.

Martha was sitting on the edge of the bed, examining the tiled floor as if it was an abyss she was considering jumping into.

'I'm not good at goodbyes,' she said. 'I object to goodbyes, you know that. I mean come on, coffee and cake? I don't want cake, I want to get out of here.'

I took Martha's hand. Together we made our way down the dark stairs, stepping over piles of dirty bed linen on the way, and into the little breakfast room, where Kurt was sitting with Francesca at a laid table, conflicting emotions flitting across his face: happiness, sadness, guilt, and confusion as to which of these responses was appropriate.

Martha kissed her father on the forehead. 'Don't get up,' she said as he tried to pull himself up into a hug. But with his remaining strength, he managed to stand up quicker than she could get away. He pulled her to him and seemed to want to whisper something in her ear, but changed his mind at the last moment.

'I'll phone you,' was all he said.

Martha nodded and disappeared out the door with a hasty 'See you later!' She always said, 'See you later,' even when it was clear she wouldn't be seeing someone for months.

I hugged Kurt too. Under his breath, he asked me to take care of his daughter, as if I were the right person for that job. Francesca gave me her hand and half a cake. I could smell the liqueur through the tinfoil.

'See you later!' I said too, in the dark knowledge that I'd never see either of them again.

Martha turned around one last time, shouting a final farewell through the open window. We drove off, and ahead of us lay Lake Maggiore. The fog had lifted, the clear sunlight fell on the mountaintops, and we could see three tiny islands in the water. The vista was surreally beautiful, the kitschiest nature had to offer, and it was obviously more than Martha could take.

She bashed her head against the dashboard, twice, three times, and the glove compartment burst open and smacked into her lips. A drop of blood oozed out, a tiny pang compared to the pain that was just beginning now and would never go away.

I pulled into the next parking space. We sat there for half an hour, didn't get out, didn't look at the back seat, didn't cry, didn't speak, until I asked:

'Shall we head home, then?'

'I can't go home now,' Martha said. 'What am I supposed to do there, apart from wait?'

She turned around to face me.

'Let's go to thingy. What's the place called again?'

'What place?'

'You know, The Trombonist.'

'Bellegra?'

She nodded.

'Might as well, I suppose, seeing as we're here anyway.'

Life's Not Much Fun Either

Martha wanted to drive; anything to keep herself from thinking. She needed to distract herself with road markings and crash barriers, she said, with labyrinthine intersections and hairpin bends. Most things Martha did in life were done to forget something else. I'd never met anyone who'd taken up as many obscure things as she had: sports with names I could never remember, instruments no one plays and no one wants to hear, languages no one speaks. She rarely got past the beginners' course, was innately geared towards the beginners' course. She had a hazy idea about everything but never truly mastered anything, and she was perpetually amazed by what she encountered. Since the accident, though, something had changed inside her, inside us all. We'd realised it was possible to fall into a fatal collision. We'd learned that no one could save us. We were in shock; we walked away with concussion, Henning with a broken arm, Martha with whiplash and Jon a mutilated face. It was his face, the most beautiful of all our faces, an actor's face, that was slashed open by the shattered windscreen. Deep down we feared he'd never recover, yet we refused to believe it. We told ourselves the scars would open the door to the underworld, the perfect face for a villain, but Jon never ventured back in front of the camera, nor Martha behind the wheel. Until today. Until she resolved to drive away from herself.

I didn't say that the winding roads by the lake probably weren't the best place to start again all these years later. I just kept driving, promising we'd swap at the next petrol station. In the meantime, Martha swiped her way through Italy on Google Maps, muttering the usual expletives, asking the deathless questions of where the hell we were and why the dot was moving in the wrong direction.

'Eight hundred kilometres to Bellegra,' she said, reading out the names of the cities on our route: Genoa, Florence, Lucca, Siena, Pisa, Orvieto. Italy was like America. It all felt familiar: names, photos, stories, holiday villas. I'd never been interested in Italy, home to a grave I was afraid to visit. And now the country to which Martha would lose her father. It was as if someone had decreed Italy *the* place to die.

'I've never been to Italy before,' she admitted.

I felt a wave of anger that we'd never been here as kids, never even seen the Adriatic coast, that in fact my Italian father had refused to set foot in this country. As West German children, this was a major omission in our cultural socialisation, but until now, we'd never felt the need to rectify it.

Martha had always assumed she'd come here when she was old, she said. Even cripples can visit Italy, she'd told herself. And now here we were.

She swiped across her iPhone again and decided we should drive to Genoa first, spend the night there, then pass through Florence and continue on to Bellegra.

'I've always wanted to go to Genoa, actually,' she said. 'Even before we found out it was where my father drank away his first heartbreak.'

I wasn't quite sure who was driving who, whose goodbyes and memories we were headed towards.

'So what are we going for here?' I asked. '*Thelma and Louise?*'

'They were young, sexy and downtrodden,' Martha said. 'Look at us, we're not even downtrodden.'

I tried again. '*Why We Took the Car?*'

'They were teenage boys. We're premenopausal women. I don't quite see the comparison.'

The countryside around us had become more tranquil. We were driving through Italy's orderly north, past turnoffs to Milan and Turin, towards the sea. Martha leaned back.

'I have to wonder how many times it's possible to lose a father,' she said. 'Even as a kid, I thought I'd never see him again. Every time we said goodbye, I'd say to myself: Let's see if he ever shows up again. Sometimes I wouldn't hear from him for months. When he eventually surfaced, we'd go for a Chinese and have no idea what to say to each other. Then he got married again. And now along comes this slapper from Lake Maggiore.'

'The woman is over seventy,' I said.

'Once a slapper, always a slapper.'

Personally, I saw in Francesca the most honest embrace anyone could hope for at the end of their life. No self-consciousness, no phoney concern. She was just there, with no apologies for not having been there the previous fifty years. It wasn't about love, it was about solace.

'Hear that?' Martha nodded her head in time to the clicking noise, which had returned. 'I need a beer,' she said with a bitter laugh.

***

While I tipped another three litres of oil into the car, Martha downed a beer. She'd lined her stomach a few minutes earlier by bolting down a pizza in Autogrill. She wanted neither to get drunk nor to remember. She just wanted to drive, to use her pain to wrench out an old trauma.

Now she was standing by the open driver's door, tugging nervously at her clothes. I had far more faith in her than she did. It was the bedrock of our friendship, our ability to believe in each other when we'd lost the strength to believe in ourselves.

'Come on,' I said. 'Your driving can't be any worse than mine.'

Martha sat in behind the wheel, adjusted the seat and mirror like a learner driver and took a deep breath. Then, without hesitation, summoning all the force she needed to set herself free, she stamped on the pedal and brought us at a demonic speed back out onto the A26 in the direction of Genoa.

At that moment, she really did seem to leave Kurt behind her, and Jon, and her guilty conscience, the experience and the harm she felt she'd done.

'You're doing great,' I said, but it was all I could do not to grip the handle above my window. As we hurtled down the left-hand lane, Martha started to sing, her voice loud, deep and sweet. I hadn't heard her sing in years.

Martha sang when she was afraid, a habit I thought unique to her until I once found myself on a plane plunging towards the earth. As we nosedived, every fourth passenger started to sing. A fragmented chorus of fear, a discordant canon swirled through the cabin, dying out when something resembling stability returned and we started to make our way upwards again. I still heard this choir sometimes when I was scared and I hadn't yet figured out why. It had become a harbinger of fear.

I averted my eyes from Martha and the road and instead fiddled with our route on the iPhone. My finger made one wrong tap and a voice came on, the one that's supposed to sound discreet and friendly but in fact just sounds pissy.

'Hazard in five hundred metres,' it said.

Martha gave a start. Ahead of us, the traffic swarmed.

'Hazard in three hundred metres.'

'What's she talking about? The exit?' Cursing, Martha tried to snatch the phone from me.

'Reduce your speed.'

'Turn it off!' Martha shouted.

'I don't know how.'

'Turn it off! That thing doesn't tell me what to do.'

I clicked and swiped.

'We just have to get to know the sat nav,' I said in an attempt to calm her down. 'Everyone should go for at least one beer with their sat nav.'

'Throw it out the window, Betty!'

'It's your phone!'

'Then take out the fucking card. We're lucky enough to belong to the generation that can still read maps.'

'Reduce your speed.'

Martha was right, the sat nav was no help. The sat nav was overanxious, the sat nav was scared. I closed the entire program. It was a relief.

In the glove compartment I found an unused map of Europe, on which Yugoslavia appeared as a single, peaceful state. This map knew nothing of wars or disputes. It exuded innocence. Underneath the map, and just as innocent, was an Adriano Celentano CD, one of his sixties' albums. By the second song, Martha was singing along, while I – in what for me was the ultimate expression of enthusiasm – nodded in time with the music. It was the closest I'd get to belting out 'Ciao Ragazzi Ciao'. Meanwhile, Martha drove as if she'd just learned to walk.

It felt like we'd stolen the car, which was far better than inheriting it: it made us feel in control again, less beholden to death. For a moment, freedom had us back, or we had it back, I wasn't sure which.

***

We approached Genoa on dual carriageways that seemed to have coiled themselves around the city. The sea glinted for a second before disappearing again behind tower blocks, and my sense of direction, poor at the best of times, got left behind entirely in umpteen curves.

We spiralled into the city, the traffic propelling us forwards from all sides, and I felt like I was in a Matchbox car, like I was at the mercy of momentum. An endless-seeming tunnel, a scrap of light, another tunnel, and then a third one, disguised as a bridge, passing right through the middle of a building. We'd booked a room online half an hour earlier, in a hotel that was just about the right side of too cheap. Olympia, it was called.

It was located right in the middle of town and promised us a space in an underground car park. I craved a parking space more than a bed.

'There's no reception,' I said every time we entered a new tunnel. 'The dot's gone. I don't know where we are.'

'Left or right after the tunnel?' Marth asked each time.

'I don't know. I can't see us any more.'

As the number of tunnels dwindled, roundabouts started appearing in their place. The sat nav kept spinning us through the city until finally Martha braked, stopped and got out of the car. Around us, demented Italians honked and gesticulated.

'That's it,' she said. 'I give up.'

I had no choice but to slide over and take the sweat-drenched wheel. We were very nearly there. That's the thing about giving up, it's so tempting to do it right before the finish line. Martha navigated us down two or three backstreets, past mountains of rubbish, and just as a gap opened up between the black sacks, she shouted, 'There!'

'What?'

'The car park. There's the entrance.'

'That's a car park? It looks like we'll be told to hand over 100,000 euros in unmarked bills down there.'

'What can I say, it's Genoa. We've arrived.'

She pointed at a decrepit neon sign on the wall. *Coin* it said, and *Coin* was what it said in our booking. There was nothing for it but to drive down. As we folded in the side mirrors, I secretly wished Martha would just push the car down with me in it, but I didn't want to show weakness. So I drove into the stinking pit, scraping the walls all the way down, and with one last groan, I parked. Twenty-four hours for 35 euros. It was pitch dark, yet there were cameras everywhere.

We bought the ticket two storeys up at a booth with smudged glass, from a couple who made it clear that they resented the interruption. Ten monitors glared behind their rumpled hair. On a building on the other side of the street, just below the roof, hung the crumbling letters *Olympia*.

The Vietnamese receptionist jangled his massive keys as though he were about to open a centuries-old portal. Italy's entire budget hotel industry seemed to have been taken over by Asians. Or in all probability they just sat behind the reception desks. The only exception was Hotel Elena, still run by Francesca – a woman, a family business.

With a highlighter, the receptionist marked two streets between the centre and the port and warned us to avoid them, especially after dark. I liked having destinations I was supposed to avoid when I was abroad. I'd already squandered my innocence in St Pauli anyway. There was no stopping me from doing things I knew were bad for me.

We strolled past drug dealers, whores and petty criminals. On this street, at least, Genoa seemed to be the same place Kurt had been so fond of. Maybe his affection stemmed from the fact that he'd had his first complete meltdown here, his only real lost weekend. Afterwards, he became a husband and a father, and shortly after that he was divorced and paying child support. Yet for all its grottiness, the street was picturesque, like a UNESCO heritage site. To me, it just looked clichéd, the perfect foil for scenic Italy: every Tuscany needs a seedy alley in Genoa. Martha didn't seem too impressed either.

'Hmm,' she said, and we were both a little disappointed that no one even tried to snatch our handbags. To console ourselves, we ordered Aperol spritzes, something we would never do back home, because home was Kreuzberg and we weren't basic. We were saving basicness for old age, when we wouldn't have much else to do.

We were sitting in a small square where four bars blended into one, a tangle of aluminium chairs and tables with a fountain in the middle that smelled like a swamp. I wondered how many of these things we'd have to drink to get through this day, a day that felt more like a chapter of our lives.

'Does your mother know you want to visit his grave?' Martha asked.

'My mother thinks every man who's left her is a loser and she wants nothing more to do with them.'

'That's a healthy enough attitude, I suppose.'

'I used to wonder how many fathers I could lose. I mean, you'd never dream of it these days: dragging home one new dad after another, each one vanishing into thin air as soon as the kid gets used to him, as soon as she really needs him. Considering my upbringing, I think I'm pretty well adjusted.'

'I'm not so sure,' Martha said. 'It's been years since you fell for a man who's actually available. And you seem to be incapable of falling in love without leaving a trail of destruction. They've all been married or else sick. Alcoholism, depression, Asperger's. There's always something. You can't fall in love unless you have an enemy to fight, and in the end, you're left with no strength to fight for love itself. I don't know anyone who falls in love so often without believing in it.'

'I can't help it, it's my age,' I said and ordered two more Aperols. They were on me, I said.

We drank like we hadn't done in years, until we forgot, until we believed we finally understood ourselves again. In Genoa, the fountains glimmered, the streets emptied, and though we couldn't see the port, we could smell it. We smelled the sea, a mixture of sewage and freedom.

***

Martha had gone outside to phone Henning. I watched her smoking in front of the window, the first time in years she'd had a morning cigarette. As usual, she'd moved out of earshot. I wasn't allowed to listen in to their conversations, as if Henning and I were two separate worlds, two rivals who couldn't be allowed in the same room.

Henning thought I was a bad influence, and I thought he was the best thing that had ever happened to Martha. Ten times I'd persuaded her to stay with him. Ten times she'd tried to leave him, always in June, usually on a Friday. It had become a little tic that no one took seriously apart from her. Just as we were getting used to this rhythm of fleeing and returning, she stopped. She seemed to have got the better of herself.

Outside, Martha squinted into the light. When she nodded, she tipped her head in such a way that I could tell, even from a distance, that she wasn't remotely interested in whatever Henning was saying on the other end of the phone.

I knew Henning thought this trip with me was a bad idea. There was no shaking his conviction that I intended to abduct Martha, to take her to some kind of dark side, as if that was my destination, as if I myself was the darkness he wanted nothing to do with. Since Jon had vanished from his life, and from our lives too, Henning had kept away from abysses. Jon was the only abyss he'd known personally, and Henning probably believed that if he stayed in his room from now on, he'd be safe, him and everyone else. Henning was someone who could sense the darkness outside and the danger in others. There was a purity in him I couldn't even imagine. In my arrogance, I used to mistake it for naivety. But Henning knew exactly what and who to keep away from. The fact that I was among them deepened my hopelessness.

Martha and I decided to get through the country as quickly as we could. Our destination lay ahead, tragedy was close behind. Wedged between fathers, memories and death, we thought we could defeat it all if we just drove faster. We'd have time after, Italy would still be there after, it was never too late to visit Italy. We were in no danger of missing some golden age; the country had been conserved for tourists several decades ago, if not centuries. The odd attraction was crumbling thanks to the financial crisis, villages were being ravaged by earthquakes, oil spills were threatening heritage sites, but otherwise it would still be there.

We'd gun it down the A1, we said, or the 'Autostrada del Sole' as they call it, spoiled braggarts that they are. We'd drive slightly less than 600 kilometres southwards, tearing through Tuscany, Umbria and Lazio without visiting a single thing. We'd see these regions only on road signs, every town an untaken exit.

Kurt told us to have fun. He hadn't said much else on the phone, hadn't been able to, Martha said; too much coughing, too little air. We sat in the car, staring at the empty back seat. It looked lonely.

'Why don't we pick up a hitchhiker?' I suggested.

'There aren't any hitchhikers left,' she said. 'They died out when the internet arrived.'

'True. I haven't seen one in ages. Shame. I'm in the mood for a hitchhiker today.'

'We need to get out of here first.'

We peered through the windscreen into the narrow, gloomy car park. The exit comprised a steep ramp with a ninety-degree bend and a barrier in the middle.

'How are we going to manage this?' Martha asked from the driver's seat.

'We'll fold in the mirrors, then I'll stand by the barrier and stick in the ticket just as you're driving up. One fluid motion and we're out.'

'Sure,' she said, and I walked up the ramp, which seemed to narrow even further as I reached the middle. I stuck up my two thumbs before any misgivings could set in. Slowly, Martha approached the ramp, and we nodded at each other as if we were at the starting line of the Dakar Rally, one of our greatest dreams back when we'd just emerged from puberty and thought anything was possible. We'd wanted to be champion race-car drivers, and now, twenty years later, we couldn't even get out of a northern Italian car park.

I shoved in the ticket, Martha revved the engine, the barrier rose, and with a single, stuttering movement she took the bend, undeterred by the wall scraping the entire length of the passenger side. Deep in concentration, she showed no reaction to the shrill, even grating sound. I ran around the bend and jumped into the car.

'We did it!' she said.

'Yeah, you did great. You did have a bit of space to your left, though.'

'Never mind, just a bit of metal. What's a car without a few scratches? I've baptised it.'

'So what have you named it?'

'You decide. Giving cars names is moronic if you ask me. Right or left?'

'Right,' I said, because I thought we should turn left. I always tried to trick my dreadful sense of direction by taking the opposite of what I thought was the right way.

As we approached an intersection, we realised that what had looked in the distance like an eight-lane road in fact had no lanes at all. Hundreds of cars were roaring across the tarmac as if a starting gun had just been fired.

'Left,' I said, and this time I was deadly certain.

Behind us we heard the squealing brakes, honking and cursing that accompany every foreign driver on Italian roads. We gestured our gratitude in all directions as we jolted our way through the unfamiliar city, Martha singing 'Azzurro' over and over until we got onto the motorway, where she eventually calmed down.

She'd been ruminating, she said, hadn't slept a wink all night, imagining what death must be like.

'Life's not much fun either,' she said. 'I mean, most of the time it's all right, I suppose, but God it grinds you down sometimes.

My family's always been a bunch of cowards when it comes to suffering. But death is silence: no more reactions, no justifications, no pain. Maybe it's a relief. I don't think anyone fights death for their own sake, they just don't want to leave others behind on their own.'

She looked over at me, and I got the sense that she wanted me to promise never to leave her. What had upset her most over the past few months was that Kurt didn't seem to care whether he lived or died. He'd refused to go to hospital, refused treatment, refused hope, however fleeting.

'I'm beginning to understand Kurt,' she said. 'I mean, all the energy, all the struggling – what would be the point? Standing by and watching him fight would probably be even worse than this. I'm sure I'd end up wishing he'd give up, just go. You shouldn't have to prove anything to anyone when you're dying.'

Martha's phone rang, and the name 'Petra' appeared on the screen. 'You answer it,' she said.

Her mother had always had a good instinct for the worst possible moment. Some people are like that, always calling at the wrong time. They can't help it but you resent them nonetheless. Bad timing has destroyed many a relationship, and it's stopped even more from getting started in the first place. I answered the phone and put Petra on loudspeaker.

She wanted to know if he was dead. If it had all 'gone smoothly', as she put it. She was crying. Mothers were strange, especially for us, because we also knew them as ex-wives stuck in never-ending failing relationships with our fathers. We'd chained together two people who wouldn't have exchanged a word in over thirty years were it not for us, and rightly so. We hadn't asked them to stay in touch, yet with every year we felt guiltier. Who wants to spend their life being a link? Some have it even worse; they're cement from the moment they're born.

It took Petra a while to grasp what we were telling her. The crying stopped and was replaced by incredulity, then outrage.

'But you can't just leave him there!' she shrieked. 'You can't just leave him behind like that!'

'You're one to talk!' Martha shouted into the phone in my hand.

'That was completely different!'

'Who's been looking after him all this time? You dumped me with a sick, lonely father who can't even afford his own nappies.'

'You've been giving him money?'

'Of course I've been giving him money. Who else has he got?'

'He tried to get out of paying child support when you were a kid, you know!'

'Well, it was you who walked out on him.'

'Oh I see, so it's all my fault? Of course it is, I'm always the villain.'

'I can't listen to you two going on about whose fault it is any more, I'm sick of it. It's your crisis, your fault. I'm just the daughter. And I work really hard at it.' Martha was now racing down the motorway at a terrifying speed.

'You make it sound like a job.'

'It certainly feels like one.'

'I see, so you handed in your notice. That really takes the biscuit, Martha, abandoning your father there with a complete stranger.'

'She's not a complete stranger.'

'Isn't she? Had you met her before? How long have they been carrying on? So much for being lonely! Poor daddy all alone in the world, tugging at your heartstrings with one hand and stuffing his nappy full of money with the other. I'll tell you one thing: he hasn't changed a bit.'

I stroked Martha's thigh. It reduced our speed by 10 kilometres per hour and the rattling subsided.

'Why are you telling me all this? He's stolen a few more days for himself, a few weeks at most. He wanted to be with her, and he didn't want me to stay. I honestly think she's the best option.

She seems like a decent, honest woman,' Martha said, in what appeared to be an attempt to reassure herself.

'I've never even heard of this woman! Where did she suddenly spring from?'

'Apparently she was on the scene before you.'

'He's got some nerve. It's disgusting! What is he thinking? At his age!'

I turned the phone away from Martha, and Petra's rant bounced off the windscreen. Martha's voice had risen now too.

'Get a grip, Petra! You can't spend the rest of your life being jealous of everyone. Of him, because you think I love him more, of this woman, who you don't even know but who's kind enough to take care of your ex-husband in his final few days. God knows why, but she's doing it. Which is more than I can say for you.'

'I looked after him for long enough! He couldn't even fry an egg back then. He would've starved to death without me!'

'And I nearly starved to death with you,' Martha said.

'We had no money, I had no choice but to work in the pub every night!'

It sounded like this wasn't the first time she'd had to justify herself. No doubt Petra had spent years of her life justifying herself. My own mother was an example of how life could turn into one long self-justification. I often got the impression she only tried to be happy so that she could furnish it to others: happiness as incontrovertible proof that she'd made the right decisions. Because what's the point of all this striving if in the end you're left sad and alone? If everything you thought you wanted is not what you needed? If what you called freedom turns out to be an aimless series of mistakes, if you yourself have become a mistake?

'I've always loved you more than anything, Martha, you know that. I'm your mother. You've always been the most important thing in my life.'

'So you say!'

For a moment Petra was silent, an all too brief moment.

'Have a kid yourself, then you can talk to me about mother-hood!' she screamed. 'You can't even manage that much!'

The car ahead of us was coming closer and closer. Martha kept heading straight towards it, showing no signs of braking. She didn't seem to have seen it; her face was frozen.

I turned the phone around again and ended the call with my index finger, a tiny movement to avert a catastrophe. The motion flowed into Martha's foot, and she stepped on the brake with such force that we jerked forwards and the seatbelts engaged with a loud click. The road behind us was clear, luckily for us.

'The woman is impossible,' she said. 'What did I do to deserve a mother like that?'

I couldn't give her an answer. We didn't deserve our mothers, hadn't done anything to earn them. We'd never earned much of anything, least of all our pasts, which through no fault of our own had plunged us into the red.

'She manages to take even her ex-husband's death personally,' Martha said. 'It's unbelievable. She takes everything as an affront.'

Without taking a breath, Martha enumerated the fights her mother had picked, the friendships she had wrecked, the jobs she'd quit, the parties, clubs and cliques she'd joined and left. And now this long-running battle with the world had presented her with the biggest affront of all: old age.

All of this spurted out of Martha at such speed that I could barely read the signs and arrows warning us of the approaching intersection. I'd thought it was easy, that we could just keep going straight ahead, but there was no straight ahead, so I decided on a road bearing right, where there'd been a sign for Florence. We had a clear division of labour: Martha drove and talked, I navigated and listened. That's the secret to a good marriage. It had once been our plan B. We'd agreed that if we didn't find anyone, we'd marry each other. When we were old we could pool our meagre pensions, we'd said, and then at least if one of us died, whoever was left would have enough to get by.

But things had turned out differently. Martha had Henning, and I had no hope of ever getting a pension. I didn't even get to be a bridesmaid because Henning wanted someone who believed in marriage, not someone who took the piss out of weddings, drank all the champagne and scrawled feminist quotes by Paula Ettelbrick in cards:

Marriage is a great institution ... if you like living in institutions. Congratulations! Betty.

Still, it had been a good party. It was the first and only time I met Martha's mother, who thought weddings were a wonderful thing, probably even salvation itself.

'Betty,' Martha said, dragging me from my thoughts. 'Are you sure this is the right way? Everything looks so small.'

'I think it looks pretty.'

'Just because it's pretty doesn't mean it's right. You would expect the A1 to be bigger.'

'The sign said Florence.'

'The other sign said Florence too.'

'What other sign?'

'The one pointing left.'

'Well, then, we can't go wrong,' I said with as much conviction as I could muster, because it did feel like something was amiss. A road with just two lanes, a strip of tarmac surrounded by fields.

We kept driving. There was no other option so we decided to just keep going until we reached another sign, until we were offered a new destination.

'Seriously though, where did I go wrong?' Martha asked. 'Why do I have this constant nagging feeling that I'm not good enough?'

I reckoned we were the first generation of women who could do whatever they wanted. But that meant we had to do what we wanted, which in turn meant we had to want something. That's what our mothers had fought for. We were expected to achieve our dreams, we were expected to have dreams. Failure was permitted, but only after we'd tried everything, absolutely everything including psychoanalysis, on the road to happiness. Giving up wasn't an option, nor was settling for less. Not with all our opportunities. My mother was always going on about them, all these incredible opportunities I had.

'"You can achieve anything you set your mind to,"' I said.

'Were you constantly being told that too? That was my mother's mantra. It's about the only thing she taught me. You can achieve anything you set your mind to.'

'Yeah,' Martha said. 'And now she's offended I haven't made her a grandmother. She puts on this sad face and shrugs her shoulders when she tells me about other people's grandkids.'

'My mother always says: "The main thing is you're happy."'

At this, Martha laughed for the first time since we'd set off. She couldn't stop. Tears streamed down her face and mine. There was no one else in the world with whom I could laugh so up-roariously at misfortune. It was one of the things I loved about her. So few women laugh at misfortune, least of all at their own. Women will talk about their misfortune until they weep, until all hope is lost. A stereotype, sure, but one I've seen confirmed a hundred times. When it comes to suffering, women have no sense of humour.

My mother couldn't fault me when it came to happiness. I was continually concocting stories about how happy I was to keep her satisfied – with me, with herself, with how she'd brought me up. She believed everything I told her, always had.

Petra hadn't been free until her own mother died, Martha said. That's when she could finally stop fighting for approval. Petra still felt guilty about how happy she was after her mother died.

'I don't know, Betty,' Martha said. 'If things keep going like this, will we have achieved anything really?'

'We'll have achieved our mothers' dreams,' I replied. 'The little ones, at least. Look at us, we're driving through Italy!'

'Yeah, we're driving through Italy because we have to see to our fathers, their cast-off husbands.'

'Well, that's about all we'll inherit from our mothers.'

I looked out the side window and saw a picture-postcard emerge on the horizon. A sight everyone knows, a sight some call a wonder of the world.

'Look,' I said. 'We went wrong somewhere.'

Martha turned her head and couldn't believe what she saw. On the horizon, in all its unreality, was the Leaning Tower of Pisa.

'It's tiny,' she said. 'Like a replica in an amusement park.'

'That's it all right. I can say with some confidence that we're not in Florence.'

'Do you want to go visit? Seeing as we're here anyway.'

'Nah,' I said. 'We can see it from here.'

'Good. Done.'

We ticked Pisa off in our heads. You don't get to know a country by looking at its sights, anyway. You get to know a country in its pubs, by bumming around in the sticks or some suburb. You get to know a country in the places where there's nothing to see. So the best places to get to know Italy are at a toxic waste dump or the container terminal in Naples. But we weren't here to get to know Italy, we were only driving through. We were just looking for the motorway.

It's not the case that road trips are full of surprises, the promise of love, sex or crime waiting at each service station. Road trips are only like that in films and novels, stories of personal growth set in the fast lane. Life is slow. It takes us years to recover from a broken heart, while on the screen, any old ape can save or destroy the world in a few days if it just believes in itself.

Maybe it was our age. At forty, surprises had lost their appeal. We were too tired to chase adventure. We'd had adventures when we were younger, and they had led to catastrophe, poverty, the occasional moment of happiness. We didn't regret any of it but we no longer felt we had to do stuff just so we could say we'd done it. We'd got used to the slight tinge of sorrow that accompanied our tiredness. We just kept going, stopping for fuel every now and then. That's life. For most people, fuel stops take the form of package holidays, cruises, love affairs. In the end, you could die from a snakebite during an Ayurvedic retreat, in a car accident in London, in a terrorist attack on a golden beach, despite never having done anything really wrong in your whole life.

A Grave in Bellegra

The name had been lodged in my brain for almost a decade. Bellegra, a word that had become a promise, a chance at redemption. That's where you were and that's where you'd stay.

We'd bypassed Florence, ignored Pisa, Siena, Orvieto and Rome to our right, taking rural roads through Lazio, a region that wasn't pretty enough for tourists, too hard to get to, the sea too far away, the mountains too low. A region inhabited by people who were tied there, whether by family, tradition, a lack of other options or an absence of ambition. A rough, unprepossessing place that didn't pay much attention to its appearance. If we spotted a single German in a straw hat here, I told Martha, I'd down a bottle of grappa in one.

I'd resumed the wheel and she was dozing in the passenger seat. For the first time since we set out, she looked relaxed, though her hand was still clamped around her phone, a device that could bring nothing but bad news. As long as it remained silent, all was well. The town greeted us with a bus station and an establishment named 'Belvedere' that claimed to be a bar but was more reminiscent of a kiosk gone awry. Rarely had I experienced such a cheerless welcome. I parked at the bus stop and went into the bar to enquire about a hotel.

I didn't understand the answer. There were a lot of words, an awful lot of words, in a language that sounded familiar but wasn't, a beautiful imposter whose intentions were unclear. What I did understand, though, was the barman's gestures: his hands, his arms, his entire body a winding upwards motion, a vertical squiggle. That must be the way. Somewhere up in that direction we'd find vacant beds.

We took the only road wide enough to accommodate a German car. All the shops were shut and the streets were deserted apart from some old men sitting in front of the church. They raised their jaded eyes as we drove past, turning their stiff necks to watch us go by like a missed opportunity.

Ahead of us, the road forked, the branch to the left leading back downhill, the one to the right winding steeply upwards. With the engine roaring and my breath held, I took the latter and followed it until it came to an abrupt stop in front of some iron railings.

Martha and I got out of the car. There was no name, no sign, just a house on top of the hill. The building was small but its location turned it into a palace. We trekked up an endless-seeming path, our footsteps crunching ominously on the gravel. The only other sound was my panting, and I felt ashamed in front of myself, in front of Martha. Martha, who was getting herself ready for a child, preparing her body to withstand any pain, rendering it safe for habitation. She'd never been as healthy as she was now, at thirty-nine.

I trod more decisively and loudly on the gravel. I'd never give up smoking, just as I'd never given up anyone or anything that caused me harm. When I looked up again, we'd reached the highest point in the town, a terrace with a view of the valley that went on for miles. At that very moment, the sun was sinking behind the mountains in the distance.

'Wow,' Martha said.

'Indeed,' I answered.

We were both trying to avoid the word 'beautiful'. It was too beautiful to be called 'beautiful'. Martha slung her arm around my shoulders.

'Not too shabby,' she said.

For a moment, it felt as if we'd arrived. It's the feeling that peaceful places can evoke after dreadful times: a sense of having arrived. You have to breathe it in deep and hold it because it wanes as soon as you exhale. It might return later with your first glass of wine, but then it dissipates entirely and the never-ending race resumes.

The hotel had two apartments and four double rooms, all of them vacant. The season was brief and far off. The Romans would come in midsummer, fleeing the heat. The landlady reminded me of Francesca, probably about the same age – except she looked it. We'd woken her up and she was now standing in front of us in her dressing gown, her face pale, her hair flat, no trace of a smile. I doubted she'd smiled once in her entire life.

She'd get a double room ready, she snapped, that was all she could offer. Then she sent us down to Sergio in the village, where there was pizza, she said, nothing else today for miles around, just pizza. It was one of the few words we understood of the hundreds repeated at breakneck speed and an extremely high volume. But I got the gist: we were to fuck off.

We were well practised in fucking off. Martha led the way down into lanes belonging to neither a village nor a city, but to what I would have to call a 'town', because I refused to refer to it as a 'small town'. Because a man of *his* stature does not come from a 'small town'.

We descended the steps into darkness. Between the buildings it smelled of must and old age, and I suspected the only reason they'd strung their laundry up outside was to mask the stink. Televisions blared and children screamed, the noise of family life behind the windows doing battle against the silence of the lanes. We kept going downhill until we reached the one restaurant where the lights were on. A man who had to be Sergio looked up from behind a smouldering charcoal oven and greeted us with a handshake. We were his only customers. We dithered in the middle of the restaurant, unable to decide on a table. Eventually Martha chose one in a corner right at the back, where she sat with her back up against the wall, as if she needed the support.

'God, what a lonely spot,' she said. To me it seemed both aloof and needy, like someone who'd been on their own for too long.

I noticed how hard I was finding it to talk in this town, how banal my words seemed as soon as I said them out loud. There was a finality about this place that, despite my having known about it for so long, had thrown me off balance.

Dumb and famished, we sat opposite each other, studying the pictures above our heads of half-naked women and erupting volcanoes. Martha brushed her hand across the checked tablecloth, one of her oldest nervous habits, an attempt to smooth out her inner turmoil.

'I hope she fries Kurt a steak,' she said. 'He likes steak.'

I placed my hand on hers and we brushed across the rough fabric together.

Sergio brought us pizza capriccioso, and it seemed right then like the best thing we'd ever tasted. 'Mmm,' Martha said quietly after her first bite. It's always the same when you're abroad, especially in the south, where everything has the potential to be a revelation, where you lose all self-restraint, dragging home memories that start to go off during the journey back. Martha examined the label on the wine bottle.

'It's from here,' she said. 'Cesanese.'

'Never heard of it,' I replied. 'Probably too vile to export and they have to drink it all themselves.'

She responded that this was another of my gross exaggerations and then asked if I'd rather be alone.

'In general, you mean?'

'No. In general, you are alone, Betty. I mean here, now?'

I didn't know.

'Well,' I said, 'it might be nice to have some time to myself tomorrow. Just a few hours. This stuff, it's between ...'

'Between you and him. I get it.'

'More between me and me, I suspect.'

Talking to someone who left you long ago is something you do by yourself. No matter whether the other person died or dumped you, you end up talking to yourself. The one left behind always wants to talk, but unfortunately, the feeling usually isn't mutual.

In the bushes outside the window, glow-worms twinkled like laser pointers.

'Does anyone live here any more?' Martha asked.

'Sergio does,' I said.

'I mean from his family. Does he still have relatives here?'

'He never talked about them, hardly ever mentioned the town. I just remember him talking about his dead mother. She used to puff up the curtains in our living room at night. But only when he'd nodded off on the sofa, and only when no one else was around. All the windows were closed, he used to say, it can't have been the wind. I saw her, he'd tell us in the morning. Superstitious Catholic nonsense, I realise now. Probably just air rising from the radiator. And he was probably drunk. That's why he would have been sleeping on the sofa in the first place.'

'There must be someone still here,' Martha insisted.

'Someone had him buried here. But I'm not sure I want to meet whoever it was. Not sure I want to find out anything I didn't know before.'

'It might be good to find out more about him.'

'Maybe. Maybe not.'

I suddenly felt the need to defend my image of him. Me at the age of nine standing in the kitchen, pressing my head against his belly; us pushing dough through the pasta machine and then drying the spaghetti on washing lines we'd strung from wall to wall. I'd allowed nothing and no one to sully these memories, and now, for the first time in my life, I was afraid someone might tarnish my image of him, perhaps even demolish it entirely.

'This isn't healthy, Betty,' she said.

'Don't start with your "healthy" bollocks. I don't want to be healthy. I hate healthy. Healthy, sorted, neurosis-free. I'm not interested.'

'You sound like an eighteen-year-old. You're not going to die young now, Betty, you're forty. It's verging on pathetic at this stage. I mean, the man walked out on you and your mother and never bothered getting in touch again.'

'Not true,' I said. 'He left my mother, so she wouldn't let him contact her. And out of respect for her, he didn't get in touch with me either.'

Martha looked out at the glow-worms, at their glittering spectacle.

'Weird,' she said. 'They're much too early. Their timing's all off. By two months at least.'

It was demented, the performance going on out in the bushes: dozens of frantically blinking little lights.

'They're mating,' Martha explained. She knew I knew nothing about nature. 'They're actually beetles, really ugly things. They look hideous in daylight, but at night, they sparkle.'

'Just like me.' I stood up to go out for a smoke. I wanted to get a closer look at my newly found kindred spirits.

When I opened the door, they swarmed towards me and then on towards the light. They seemed disoriented as they alighted on Martha's forearm. They'd obviously gone mad. Any creature that stops being afraid of human beings has clearly lost its mind.

Martha's phone lit up as a message arrived, and one of the insects lunged at the flashing display. It was one of the sorriest sights I'd ever seen: a glow-worm trying to fuck an iPhone.

***

The next morning I stood there, alone.

There were hundreds, thousands of graves. Forty or fifty by each wall. Then there were the family plots: Famiglia Tranquilli, Rocchi, Santese.

In front of every grave, a battery-operated candle and fresh flowers. So many flowers. So many photos, stuck above the names in oval frames. More graves lined up on the ground. I was looking for your name but was afraid of seeing your photo. It had been more than twenty-five years since we'd last seen each other, and there hadn't been a single photo since, not one letter, one phone call.

I passed freshly dug – or exhumed – graves. In nearly every plot lay a husband and wife. Hardly anyone lay alone. Had you been alone? Was someone with you when you died, would someone follow you? Could I be the one who followed you? I'd like to be.

There were too many graves, I could see no end to them. Two-storey above-ground graves that looked like houses, rolling aluminium ladders and empty cans of cleaner in front of them. Little passages branched off every couple of metres, dead ends blocked by metal grilles.

I searched and searched, had to sit down for a while, couldn't make out the names any more; the dead were blurring before my eyes. Eventually I came to a little chapel with four narrow wooden benches inside. The plaster was peeling off and though there was no way the sun ever shone in here, the pictures of Jesus had faded. Three yellow plastic watering cans and an aluminium chair.

I couldn't find you.

A couple of old women were arguing somewhere, or perhaps just chatting. How would I know the difference? As I got closer, I realised that one of the women was our hotel landlady. She stared at me with surprise but no trace of friendliness, her unblinking eyes following me, piercing me. I continued walking as if there was a knife lodged between my shoulder blades.

Lizards darted across the paths, I saw marble, flowers, golden lettering, but I didn't see you. After all this time, all this waiting, you had to be here somewhere.

I'd never even got word that you'd died, never got an invitation to your funeral. The only thing I got was the letter I'd sent you, which was returned to sender. It was the first I'd ever written you. By chance I'd eaten in a restaurant whose owner turned out to be an old friend of yours. It took a while for us to place each other. You and I had been regulars in his old place, where we'd never paid for anything.

He hadn't seen you in a long time, he said. He didn't explain why, just wrote your address on a napkin and told me to give you his regards. An address in a suburb of Hamburg. The napkin lay on my desk for weeks until I finally found the first tentative words. I wasn't brave enough to simply visit you. The letter came back with a stamp: *No longer at this address.* There was no other trace of you until years later, when I learned that you'd died. My mother casually mentioned it after finding out from some old, near-forgotten acquaintances she'd run into at a party.

It took me a while to find your oldest friend, whose surname I remembered because you'd always called him by it. He told me where you were buried. Bellegra. He couldn't tell me anything else, as you'd disappeared from his life long ago too. All I had was the name of this town and the hope that it would be enough, that I'd come here one day, when I was ready. I never expected it to take me ten years. I had no idea how tenacious grief can be. I didn't know that it's not always all-consuming anguish, that it comes in bouts, creeping in and settling beneath what we call skin. A skin that doesn't get thicker with the years, just swells up slowly from inside.

I trudged past the gravestones, my strength already waning.

How I would have liked to carry your name. First I dreamt of adoption, later of marriage. Your name. And now here it was before my eyes, carved into stone.

Ernesto Carletti
6.11.1946 – 12.4.2007

Second-to-last row, third from the left. I turned away and looked into the valley. It was cold in the shade, where you lay. This plot would always be in the shade. The sun would never find its way here. Who builds something like this, a grave with no light? It wasn't right. You were the sun, and I don't care how mawkish that sounds. I was six, and you were a pot-bellied sun. There would never be another like you.

Now you were a name on a slab of marble. No picture like the others. Paths everywhere, fences everywhere, light only on the big graves. The sun was only for those who could afford it. What the hell was going on? What were you doing here?

When you moved in with us, I wasn't a kid any more, I was a six-year-old girl, and I wanted you to like me as a girl. Later, I fell in love with men who resembled you, I fell in love with the memory of you. The sense of security you gave me never returned. I found it in no one else's arms. Maybe it was for the best that you left before I grew up. What would have become of us otherwise? And yet I couldn't help imagining: what might have become of us?

God knows how it took me until my forties to figure it out. Any half-decent therapist could have told me after the first session. They pull out every malady by the roots. You go along for two years and have it talked out of you until you've no roots left, until you're not a vegetable any more, until you're liberated and capable of intimacy. But instead, here I was standing by your grave, this meaningless root made of ash and stone.

I jumped over the graves, hurried down the hill and wandered the alleys of your childhood. The town you came from and were buried in had nothing to do with us. Your story wasn't our story. I didn't exist here, and that hurt. A love that no longer had any ties.

I saw you nowhere and everywhere. You walked towards me, watched me go past. I saw you in the faces of others, sometimes as a memory in the faces of old people but more often in the faces of children who could have been yours, who could be your grandchildren or nephews. You could have been in any one of these faces because I refused to accept the alternative, that you were gone completely. I saw you in all these shadows.

Did you have children after me, your own children? Did you walk down these alleys as a young man? Did you love someone before you came to us? I never asked you, I thought we had time. Back then, I didn't know that people can vanish. You were there and that was all I needed. I didn't want to know where you came from, and I definitely didn't want to know where you were going.

You returned here as a corpse. One of the town's lost sons. My lost father. What a fuck-up you must have been.

The dead outnumbered the living in this town, and butchers outnumbered hairdressers. Everyone was called 'ragazzi' here, bald eighty-year-old women were greeted with a 'Ciao bella' and wine was sold in plastic bottles for €1.50 a litre.

And the whole time, the song you used to sing was on repeat in my head. It was horrible. A godawful pop song. You used to sing the worst Italian pop while you were cooking. Why did you do it, all of it?

The village that had brought you forth looked like a painting. You came from a fucking painting, your birthplace was romance itself. Why would someone like you subject himself to German reality?

In the tobacconist's, grandmothers rubbed out the joy, the very, very small piece of joy they had paid for with what remained of their pensions. They were squashed into the ten-square-metre shop, which sold postcards of Rome and just one of this town, the latter featuring a picture that must have been at least fifteen years old. They hunched over the tobacco in a line stretching from right inside the door to the far wall, bags of courgettes, bread and homemade salami on the floor beside them. Three-wheeled vans drove past stacked with fruit, their deals blasting from megaphones and reverberating through the alleys. From the windows, old women peered down at old men.

No one here but old folk and little kids. The young people were in Rome, earning a living. At night you could hear them talking and laughing in the distance, their voices floating up from the bus station and Bar Belvedere. By day, it was a town in its final throes, decrepit people in dilapidated houses. A privy that had been torn down decades ago, the only thing left a rusty cistern hanging on the wall, like a weed growing out of a ruin. Steps going up and steps going down, yet more steps, a glimpse of sky, laundry and pictures of the Virgin Mary. Tiny red spiders scurrying across the paving stones. They looked like measles.

I could understand why you'd left here. There were green shutters on faded buildings here, and white plastic chairs in front of the church. Every colour was watered down, peeling off. There was nothing to do here but hang laundry up outside the windows. In these narrow alleys, the longing to spread your wings was likely to overpower you. It was ready to pounce when you turned the next corner, to dig its claws into you and breathe down your neck. You couldn't breathe here. In these grey confines, it seemed possible to ossify from the inside.

Did you ever think about how things used to be? The way I did after you left? It was a merciless departure. I refused to get older, did you know that? I was twelve, and sometimes I think I haven't got any older since then, just harder. I hardened suddenly, as suddenly as I stopped growing. You went, and I stood still, with all the strength I could muster. They say I'd always been a stubborn kid. I have no memories of being a kid. All my memories begin with you.

I stood in front of an estate agent's window, which was sandwiched between a clothes shop called Mampieri and a delicatessen also called Mampieri. The words *Da vendere* were stuck to doors all over the town, the specs pasted onto windows that were brown with dirt. Behind them were empty, forgotten apartments where the elderly had stayed until they died, where unwanted furniture silently rotted, where animals found homes for the winter. The flats were going for as little as €20,000.

I'd never been rich, knew nothing about the property market, but even I could see this one had collapsed. A flat with a kitchen, bathroom, bedroom and living room for €20,000 – that wasn't cheap, it was being thrown away. I briefly considered disappearing here, hiding in this town in the mountains, in a dark, narrow alley with no natural light and a view of weather-beaten steps. The buildings were so close together it wouldn't matter which direction my flat was facing. Everyone here had to go outside if they wanted a glimpse of the sun.

The town ended on the left: a hillside plunging into a motorway, then nothing. Just mountains. I heard Mass being said somewhere but I couldn't see a church. No matter where I looked, the view ended with a wall. Everything was crumbling. Wild bushes grew out of windows, pushing their way past the few remaining slivers of glass. And satellites everywhere, the Middle Ages set to receive. Everything was called a 'piazza', even the courtyards where the dustbins were kept. The lower depths of the town surrounded me like an open grave.

***

Dark dots danced like shadows on the ceiling but otherwise the room was completely still. Lying there rigid in the bed, I knew something wasn't right. Somewhere just after the Italian border, my medication had run out. I'd planned on being back home long ago. Now I was travelling without supplies, a depressive going cold turkey.

I'd been taking a pill every day for the previous two years, slowly increasing the dose until the doctor decided I was 'perfectly calibrated'. I'd liked how he put it, I liked how he warned me several times that under no circumstances was I to abruptly stop the medication. I was to 'taper it off', he'd said. The same should apply to relationships, I'd thought. People should taper each other off, gradually reducing their doses until they can do without each other entirely.

But now I was stuck in this forlorn corner of Italy without a single tablet. This wasn't a tapering-off, it was a break-up via text message.

My mouth was full of nails, my saliva tasted metallic, my tongue was numb. Sadness between my teeth, ruining my appetite. It felt as if something inside me had ruptured and was seeping through every pore, leaching into my organs. Maybe it was all the losses I'd experienced. They were getting mixed up, and I could no longer tell where they started and I stopped.

***

'Get dressed!' Martha said. 'There's a party going on down in the town.'

She was sitting on the edge of my bed, shaking my arm. I'd no idea how long she'd been there. I'd no idea about anything: what day it was, what time, where I was or why. But I did recognise my friend Martha, who was in high spirits and giving off a strange smell.

'Come on,' she said. 'We're in Italy! There's a party with wine and bacon and fireworks!'

'They shouldn't have,' I said.

Martha had spent the whole day in Bar Belvedere trying to forget everything, to forget Kurt. Now an embodiment of pure, desperate joie de vivre, she wobbled dangerously at the edge of my bed as she tried to pull me upright.

'The next round of drinks is on the new mayor!'

'You smell weird,' I said.

Martha shrugged. 'We both stink,' she said. 'We've been wearing the same clothes for days, what do you expect? Anyway, it's not like we're in Florence or Venice. Everyone stinks here, believe me.'

'I really don't feel like going out.'

Outside the window, the clouds loomed so low and thick, it was as if the valley had gone up in flames. We up here were the last survivors, with no one to rescue us.

I told her about Ernesto's grave, about my tablets. Even I noticed I sounded addled, that I hadn't managed to transform my thoughts into sentences, that it was all very hazy. I could barely understand what I was saying myself. Martha leant down and put her arms around me, a hug we both badly needed.

'Betty, I need this right now,' she said. 'A party with people who know nothing about us and want nothing from us, who think we're just two friends driving through.'

Which was, after all, what we were.

'Get up,' she said. 'Please. You're going to lose the plot completely in here.'

My body felt heavier than usual. I heaved myself out of bed, got dressed and allowed Martha to drag me down the alleys towards the music. Even from this distance, it sent a shudder down my spine.

There was free wine in front of the town hall. Standing on a stage was the new mayor, who, despite wearing trainers with two-inch soles, can't have been much taller than 5'2". He concluded his speech by blowing kisses into the audience, upon which a mechanic with oil-smeared hands grabbed the microphone and sang Frank Sinatra covers. Kids danced, parents poured themselves wine from plastic one-gallon containers, and everywhere I looked, I saw rhinestones and spangles, jeans that managed to be simultaneously tight and saggy, faded rock stars on flimsy T-shirts, bulging bellies, neon-yellow shoes. Whoever said Italians know how to dress? The fashion sense on display here would be at home in a trailer park. It was glorious.

The mayor was now accepting *complimenti* from the crowd, kisses on both cheeks, even from Martha, who had very obviously been drinking since midday. The newly elected administration wasn't a party, she told me, but a group of young people looking to do things differently. They certainly looked young, really young, or else I'd just got really old, I wasn't sure.

The men kept looking at my hands to check whether I was off limits. I should have got myself a ring. If you go to these parties without a wedding ring, you might as well show up naked. People offered us their seats, words were flying, everyone was laughing, and everything felt wrong, because I was here without you, because you were beneath a slab of stone.

I spotted our landlady sitting in a conspicuously quiet group at the other end of the piazza. I could practically hear their silence rumbling in the distance. Everyone else seemed to keep their distance from the table, and the longer I watched the action around us, the clearer I could see the silent feuds that had probably been raging for generations. There was never outright war, people just stayed out of each other's way. That's what it's like in these small towns, I thought; everyone knows too much about everyone else.

I ate and drank everything they brought us: ham, bread, copious amounts of wine. We raised our glasses and I smiled at Martha. The giddier she got, the deeper I sank into silence. I was trying to have fun for her sake, but it wasn't working.

I said my goodbyes and thank-yous after the fireworks, while I was still able to walk in a straight line. I'd learned many lessons in life, and one of them was: eat like a man, drink like a man, and leave like a lady.

Martha gave me a tight, almost passionate hug, but at the same time there was something half-hearted about it, as is often the case with hugs from inebriated people. We'd never minded when one of us abandoned the other to the company of drunken men. She told me to get some rest, to sleep it all off, as if I might just wake up a new person the next morning. I hesitated for a moment but she'd already turned away and was laughing loudly, her cheeks flushed.

I traipsed along the narrow lanes leading up the hill, music at my back and longing in my stomach, and went to my room. From the window I could see the illuminated cemetery, the little battery-operated lights in front of every gravestone. It looked like a block of flats whose residents were still awake. I wasn't tired. I couldn't resist.

***

I was woken by the sound of mowers looping around the olive groves, hacking down the spring.

Martha was in bed beside me, fully clothed and smelling of cork. Everything about her soothed me. There was dirt underneath my nails, my fingertips were bloody, my hands scratched. I'd ventured out again the previous night. Before I had a chance to fully come to, someone started knocking on the door. This was no gentle wake-up knock, it was the hammering of a Fury, and she was screaming something that, beyond a shadow of a doubt, included the word *Polizia!*

I opened the door and Martha opened one eye. The landlady was standing outside, flapping her arms. I pointed at my barely clothed body and shut the door again.

'What's going on?' Martha asked as I pulled on my trousers.

'Police,' I said.

She sat up and squinted at me out of gummy eyes. There was something touching about her attempt to fix me with what she thought was a penetrating gaze.

'I went back to the cemetery last night,' I admitted.

'Is that against the law?'

That hadn't occurred to me. Laws, rules, decency – these categories didn't apply to me. Now, though, details were beginning to emerge from the fog. I'd climbed over the locked gate and rested my head on the grave, clawed at it, pounded it with my fists. As I filled Martha in, I began to veer so violently between shame and disgust that I had to sit down.

'I think,' she said, her tongue heavy, 'we might need the German.'

A man called Wolf had sat down beside her the night before and given her the usual spiel: the town's history, the architecture, the olive oil. He was an expert on all of it, having had a house here for decades. But when she'd asked him about Ernesto, he'd gone quiet. His only advice was not to pester the locals, especially not the older ones.

'What's that supposed to mean?' I asked.

'Don't ask me,' Martha said. 'But there's something fishy going on here.'

Downstairs, the policeman was shouting; I assumed he was ordering me to hurry up. It felt like a film where the villain doesn't have enough time to destroy the evidence, but in this case, the evidence was embedded under my nails.

'I'll ring him,' Martha said.

'Who?'

'The German. Maybe he can help us. We're going to need someone to translate, at least, unless you want to wind up in jail. All you need now is a few misunderstandings and you'll have fifty crimes on your rap sheet.'

A bit over the top, I thought, but she was right. We needed a translator.

Out on the terrace smoking was a uniformed man with jacked muscles that had turned to fat. He greeted me with a suspicious nod, at which I made it clear that I wouldn't be saying a word until this Wolf character showed up. We waited in silence as the fog rolled up towards us from the valley, our landlady looking daggers at me the entire time. There was no doubt she hated me. What was less clear was why. Sometimes you're the knife in a wound you know nothing about, bringing back memories you had nothing to do with. I glanced over and saw that her whole body was tensed, her hands gripping the armrest of her chair so tightly I felt sure she'd reached breaking point.

After an excruciating half hour, we heard the sound of panting coming from the gravel path. Wolf was a gentleman in his mid-seventies who, as Martha only revealed to me now, had once been a well-known writer, or so he said. But then a German writer is guaranteed to crawl out from under a rock no matter what godforsaken corner of the world you end up in. If this writer's ravaged face was anything to go by, he specialised in autobiographical novels. I made a mental note to get my hands on one of them when all this was over.

Not only was he wearing a linen suit, but he also sported a signet ring on his little finger and, it pains me to add, a straw hat. Though by that point I'd have been more than happy to down a bottle of grappa.

Wolf greeted our gathering with a little bow, during which I was sure I could hear his back crunch, and sat down next to Martha at the table.

Did the name Ernesto Carletti mean anything to me, the policeman began. The way he spat out the name – a name that was apparently unmentionable here – gave me pause for thought. This policeman clearly meant business, and for a second I considered denying all knowledge of you. No one would ever be able to prove a link. In effect there was no link: not a single document connecting us, and the passage of time had destroyed the last few pieces of evidence.

'Your husband?' the policeman asked. Wolf didn't look at me as he translated.

'He wasn't my husband.'

'Your father?'

'He wasn't my father.'

There was no point in denying it. No point for me, anyway. The landlady's face told me there was a lot at stake here, that there was a story I could dig up if I wanted to.

'He was the man I loved like a father,' I said. 'And the father I loved like a man.'

The policeman lit another cigarette and scribbled something in a notebook before looking back up at me.

'You desecrated his grave,' he said. 'You tried to open it with a shovel. You disturbed the peace of the dead.'

Wolf remained stony-faced as he translated. I was starting to like him. The bit about the shovel was news to me.

'Nonsense,' I said. 'The peace of the dead, please. I paid him a visit. I might have knocked a bit loudly, that's all.'

It was the only tactic I could think of: to act as if it was all perfectly normal behaviour, as if I hadn't had some kind of meltdown last night. I decided I'd sooner end up in prison than the loony bin.

Beside me, Martha gagged. No one batted an eyelid as she jumped up and ran to our room. No doubt it was a common enough occurrence in a wine town like this.

'Are you married?' he asked.

'I beg your pardon?'

'Are you married?' Wolf repeated, looking at me this time.

'I heard it the first time. No, I'm not married.'

The policeman inspected me from top to bottom, as far as it was possible with the tabletop going across the middle of my body. His gaze was relentless, boring through everything it met, registering every flaw, every bump and wrinkle.

'You should have got married while time was still on your side,' Wolf translated.

Seeing as this wasn't a question, I didn't respond.

With an air of nonchalance, the policeman placed our car registration certificate on the table.

'Where did you get that?' I asked, more loudly than I'd intended. The policeman just nodded.

'Yes,' I said. 'The car belongs to Kurt Wegener. He's my friend's father. We were taking him to a euthanasia clinic in Switzerland.'

The landlady emitted a chilling harrumph, while from upstairs came the no less chilling sound of Martha retching. 'My God, you ladies seem to have a thing for dead fathers,' Wolf translated, and I began to wonder if he was secretly embellishing the dialogue.

'He's not dead,' I said.

'Where is he then?'

'At Lake Maggiore.'

'Alive?'

'Yes. Well, I assume he's still alive. We haven't heard otherwise.'

'You left a dying man to fend for himself at Lake Maggiore? Please, help me picture the scene. Did you throw him out of the car at a service station? Or did you dump him in the lake itself?'

He stubbed out his cigarette on the middle of the table.

'No! No, we handed him in.'

'Handed in?'

'Yes, we handed him in.'

'There's a dump at Lake Maggiore where you can get rid of old, dying men?' The policeman sniggered. 'Can you give me the address? I'll pass it on to my wife, it might come in handy for her.'

'No,' I said. 'It was a private arrangement.'

'Private?'

'With an ex-girlfriend of his who lives there,' I explained.

'Holy mother of God, what kind of sordid family life do you people have in Germany?'

Wolf's impassivity suggested he heard this question on a regular basis. Only Martha succeeded in provoking a reaction from him as she staggered back to the terrace and collapsed onto a lounger. Meanwhile, the policeman leaned over the table towards me.

'Ernesto Carletti was not a good man.'

That was not what I wanted to hear. My voice was shrill as I replied that I'd loved you, that you'd been a good man to me.

'You're mistaken,' he said. 'Just ask his sister here. Not even she thought he was a good man.'

I stared at the nodding landlady. How could this harridan be your sister? She didn't bear the slightest resemblance to you. An unfamiliar feeling exploded inside me, a feeling that wasn't part of my repertoire and that was completely inappropriate in the present circumstances: never before had I experienced such fierce jealousy.

'But he didn't even live here!' I shrieked.

'You don't have to live here to cause trouble,' he said. 'Trouble can be sent.'

What I was hearing was making less and less sense. I needed my pills.

'Not only was he a bad man,' the policeman continued, 'but he was stupid too. Stupid enough to pick a fight with the wrong family.'

'What do you mean, the wrong family?' I asked.

'You must be as stupid as him,' he said with a shake of the head that both prohibited any further questions and was answer enough in itself.

'Oh, come on!' I shouted. 'What kind of place is this?'

'This is Italy, Signora Betty.'

He was completely serious. I searched Wolf's face in vain for a clue as to what on earth was going on. But Wolf just sat there motionless, like a puppet without strings.

'Is this some kind of sick joke?' I said. 'You've got to give me more than that!'

Whenever I found myself in uncharted situations, I tended to come out with sentences lifted straight from daytime TV, an embarrassing phenomenon I'd only recently become aware of.

'I'll tell you another thing,' the policeman said. 'As well as being bad and stupid, Carletti was a coward. He ran off and went into hiding. On an island. In Greece, to add insult to injury.'

'What island?' I demanded.

'I'm not at liberty to say. Investigations are still ongoing.'

'Investigations are ongoing? The man has been dead for ten years!'

'Basta!' The landlady banged her fist on the table and stood up. I noticed that I too had sprung out of my chair. It had suddenly become very quiet out here. I looked in despair at Martha. Her skin had taken on a greenish tinge; I feared she would pass out any minute now. She looked the way I felt, if for other reasons.

The policeman and I smoked a cigarette in silence and then he started all over again. He simply went right back to the start, as if nothing had been said until now.

'What were you doing at Ernesto Carletti's grave?' he asked.

'I was trying to open it,' I said, and as I was speaking the night returned to me. There had indeed been a shovel, and I had used this shovel. 'But I couldn't. It's sealed with a slab of marble. Whoever buried him must have been mighty scared of him.'

'What did you intend to steal from the grave?'

'I didn't intend to steal anything. I wanted to put something in,' I said.

'And what did you want to put in?'

'Myself.'

He rested his head on his hands and stared at me.

'Are you insane?' he asked.

'Yes,' I replied. 'I'm beginning to think I might be.'

'So what am I to do with you now?' Wolf had closed his eyes.

The fog rising from below had become so dense I could no longer see the valley. Our world ended at a palm tree. Behind it, everything was white, a bank of clouds I wanted nothing more than to jump into.

But instead, Martha arose from the lounger, climbed onto the wall, threw herself into the olive grove and rolled away. Wolf jumped up but I grabbed his flaccid writer's hand and he let me hold on to him as if he'd been waiting for this moment for years.

The policeman looked back and forth between me and Wolf, down into the olive grove and finally at the landlady, who sat in silence, her eyes cast heavenwards, either lamenting or cursing. She was probably cursing you, had probably been cursing you for years. My Ernesto.

'Can I ask you something?' he said. 'Are you two typical German women?'

'From Berlin,' I said. 'Capital city typical. We'll keep out of trouble from now on.'

The policeman shut his notebook with a sigh.

'Come to the station in the morning so I can take your details.'

'But I'm here now,' I protested. 'And so are you!'

'The computer is only on between nine and twelve on Mondays.'

All I'd wanted was to say goodbye here, to make a fresh start. Things hadn't exactly gone according to plan.

The policeman pushed his chair back under the table and took one final look into the valley, his precinct. It lay there so placid, so suspicious, it seemed to me now. Wouldn't it be normal to want to get out of here, to escape to an island? Or was I the only person normal enough to see that?

'What island?' I asked again.

'Fuck the island.'

Wolf translated stoically, pretending to have no interest in what he was hearing, but he was smuggling everything into that unimaginative novelist's brain of his, of that I had no doubt. I knew a thing or two about brains like that.

'I'll find out,' I said.

'Let me give you a piece of advice: forget him.'

I'd have needed more than two hands to count the number of times I'd received that advice. In most cases, it was good advice. It had taken months of mourning and debauchery, mournful debauchery, debauched mourning, a loneliness that stole my sleep and my sanity, self-pity that oozed out of me like pus, for me to see how well-intended that exact advice was. But in the end, everything would turn into memories, and the memories eventually faded. First, I'd forget why I'd loved these men, and later, much later, I might even forget their names. But I would never forget you. Love began with you.

We stood opposite each other on the terrace, the policeman and I, while the landlady perched on her chair, her glare still fixed on me. I'd never seen such burning hatred in such dull eyes. The woman seemed to be stitched together with ugly scars left by old wounds. She was obsessively twisting a dent on her finger where a wedding ring used to be. We were frozen in place, like art models, but there was nobody painting the scene. We were interrupted by the sound of a chainsaw pulverising the gravel path. It seemed to be making its way up at an almighty speed, and as it came towards the hotel, I saw that the chainsaw had two wheels and had been manufactured by Yamaha. Behind the handlebars was a man who I decided could only be called Enzo, and behind him a woman I knew was called Martha.

With scratches on her face and a battered olive branch in her hair, she looked like the exhumed corpse of the 1994 German Wine Queen pageant-winner. Glowing with adrenaline, she nearly toppled over as she got off the pillion. Very few people know how to dismount elegantly. She lurched towards me, her knee grazed and her shoes missing. Enzo switched off the engine before offering a brief explanation.

'She rolled from the olive grove right out onto the street,' Wolf translated.

'Mamma mia!' the landlady shrieked, shaking her head. She then proceeded to pray. Maybe Catholicism really was their only hope around here. Maybe she was in the early stages of Parkinson's and the headshaking was a result of nerve damage. Or maybe it was the DTs. What did I know? I'd disliked people who'd turned out to be sick, and I'd loved people I would have loathed had they been healthy. I'd been wrong often enough before.

Martha grabbed on to my shoulder and assured us she was fine, she'd just needed some me time.

The man I'd named Enzo blew us goodbye kisses and ploughed back down the path. The policeman then took the landlady's hand and persuaded her to go for lunch with him. Wolf took his leave too, saying he wanted to write one more poem before his afternoon nap. Had he been ten years younger, I would have attempted to save him, doubtlessly without success.

Martha and I stayed on the terrace, like the only two people left in the cinema as the final credits roll.

'It's all very odd,' Martha said.

'I have to go to that island,' I said.

'But Betty, he's dead.'

'I haven't seen him dead.'

'You were at his grave. Come on now, keep it together.'

Given the events of the previous night, this advice was a little late.

'There must be some kind of clue in her flat: a postcard, an old address, a photo, something. He was her brother after all,' I said.

'Please don't tell me you're thinking of breaking in?' I could see she already knew the answer.

'I'll stay here and keep watch,' she said.

I didn't need a shovel this time, just my health insurance card. It snapped in two and fell to the ground in front of the back door. I silently congratulated myself on not having used my credit card.

The laundry room contained stockpiles of wine in plastic bottles. It smelled of fabric softener and old woman, a cloying, slightly fermented odour. The next door was unlocked, and behind it, as I'd hoped, lay her apartment. I slipped in like a burglar, which is ultimately what I was, a thieving amateur.

The place was strewn with cheap jewellery, reading glasses scattered everywhere but nothing to read, the Virgin Mary on walls and dressers. Alongside this Mary fixation were black-and-white wedding pictures, one of them probably her own, and three colour photos of couples. She was a mother of three, then, a mother-in-law and no doubt a grandmother now too, a matriarch with grandchildren who fled her wet kisses. Which meant you had been an uncle, with nieces and nephews you'd never even mentioned, a life I knew nothing about.

I pulled open drawers, rummaged through papers and hand towels. There had to be something – a picture, a scrap of memory – but all I found were photos of grandchildren and albums of family occasions in which there was always one person missing.

I folded back the plastic accordion door leading to the bedroom and behind it, a roomful of birds stared at me. One bird after another, they were perched in every corner, on top of the wardrobe and beside the bed. Stiff, motionless birds with empty eyes, nailed to wood, dead and stuffed.

I flung open the wardrobe doors, found the real jewellery she probably never wore except to the odd baptism, and rifled through her knickers, all my scruples lost. I was interrupted by a thin, feeble whistle that could only have come from Martha. I heard the front door opening, the footsteps approaching, but I was rooted to the spot, caught in the dead birds' stare.

The landlady screamed into my face. As she showered me with abuse, her face turned so red I began to worry she'd drop dead, her veins would burst, not just under her skin but in her brain too. When she was done screaming, she grabbed me by the ear and dragged me outside. I was a woman in her forties being dragged out by the ear, and I have to admit, it hurt. She let go of me outside the front door, dropping me like a stinking rag.

***

'You should've talked to her,' Martha said. 'Just talked.'

'She didn't exactly seem to be in the mood for a chat.'

'You could have asked her about Ernesto, where he lived, what he did, what kind of trouble he was in.'

'She dragged me out by the ear, Martha!'

'You did break in to her flat. If this was America, she'd have blown your brains out. Dragging someone out by the ear is pretty quaint in comparison.'

'She called me a whore's daughter! You're the daughter of a whore, she said.'

'You don't know that.'

'My Italian is good enough to recognise a swear word when I hear one. Swear words and "I love you" are always the first things you learn. That plus a few groceries, a few numbers, please, thanks, hello, and you've got everything you need for a civilised existence.'

Martha just looked at me and shook her head.

It was becoming clear that I couldn't have bungled things more. I'd behaved like a child, perhaps because part of me had become a child again. A sad, stubborn little girl alone in the schoolyard with no one to collect her.

'I'm going back,' Martha said. 'We can't just leave it like this.' The way she stomped up the path indicated that she wanted neither dissent nor company. The only thing I could think of to do was light another cigarette and wait for a commotion to start up again in the hotel.

Minutes went by and I heard nothing, no doors slamming, no cursing, just perfect silence until footsteps crunched on the gravel again. Martha wasn't smiling but there was something triumphant about her return. In fact, there was something triumphant in her hand, which was now stretched out to me. A scrap of yellow paper with just one word on it: *Lofkes*.

'What's this?' I asked.

'Your island.'

She didn't reveal how she'd done it. Martha had always had her own methods of getting what she wanted. In this case, I suspected a deployment of hard cash rather than diplomatic skill. Still, that's a skill in itself, being able to identify the people who'll sell their secrets for money.

I was quietly cheered by the fact that I'd never heard of this island. It's the small, remote places you've never heard of – the hidden paradises nobody ever talks about because they want to keep them for themselves, because every paradise goes to shit once you share it with others – those are the places that preserve clues and stories, which was all I could hope for.

'Thanks,' I said in a low voice.

Martha responded with a smile I'd seen many times before. It was slightly lopsided, her upper lip a crooked line, and what it meant was that she didn't approve but wished me luck all the same.

We both needed a coffee and agreed it would be best to find one in the next town. It was time to get out of Dodge.

'I can't drive, though,' Martha said. 'I'm still pissed.'

'Well, I'm chemically unbalanced. Poor circulation, blurred vision, cognitive impairment, disorientation.'

'Did you learn your package insert off by heart or what?'

'I've learned myself off by heart.'

'Italy is making you histrionic.' She was right. This country relished drama, and I was susceptible to drama. Until now, I'd thought no one was aware of that apart from me.

Martha slid onto the passenger seat. My vision was frayed, everything blurred at the edges. Only in the middle was there a sharp circle, a peephole through which I'd have to find the way onwards.

'Wait,' Martha said as I turned the key. 'My phone's ringing.'
She neither picked up the phone vibrating in her bag nor got out of the car. She stayed buckled into her seatbelt, staring first at the glove compartment, then at her hands.

'My phone's ringing,' she said again.

Her movements were slow, as if she were sick, as if her body hurt everywhere. She unfastened her seatbelt, got out of the car and slowly walked away until she was out of earshot. In the rearview mirror, I watched her nod and pace, watched her body tense up and the tension turn into agitation.

She hung up and tilted her head back. Looked up at the sky, where there was no one waving back down at her, and then over at me, still sitting in the car. To her, I must have looked like a frozen image. When you hear momentous news, no matter whether it's good or bad, you turn around afterwards and find that the world hasn't moved, while for you, everything's changed. A chasm has appeared out of nowhere, a chasm that might never go away. Martha was now walking back to the car, her strides curiously long, as if she were vaulting over obstacles on her way.

'Back to Lake Maggiore,' she whispered.

'What's happened?'

'I didn't quite catch it all,' she said. 'He's doing better. He's doing well, in fact, and he wants us to come back.'

I asked whether it was Francesca who'd called, but it had been Kurt himself. He hadn't sounded this good in weeks, she said. In a faltering voice, she started talking about a miracle, said she couldn't decide who was responsible for it: Lake Maggiore, Francesca, love, the air.

Nobody is responsible for miracles. That was her first mistake. Her second was that there's no such thing as miracles, there's just one final rally, but I didn't have the heart to tell her. I generally refrain from crushing hopes that aren't my own. Instead, I started the engine and Martha's residual drunkenness burned up into euphoria.

Women Getting Out of Cars

Bellegra had disappeared behind a bend as if it had never existed, an apparition that had given me no answers, just more questions. Our fathers had never been reliable. The more we learned about them, the less we knew.

'He sounded like a different man,' Martha said. She'd never heard Kurt talk that way before; he'd sounded downright excited. 'More alive than ever,' she said, and we both laughed. Maybe the love of a good woman would actually save him. It can be so simple sometimes, but so hard to come by.

'Do you believe all that stuff the policeman said?' Martha asked. 'About Ernesto not being a good man? That business about the wrong family?'

'I don't believe anything any more,' I said, screwing up my eyes to peer into the Italian spring. 'Everything's pixelated, shitty quality. The world looks like an illegal download.'

'I've had that flickering vision thing too,' she said. 'It's stress-related. You need to relax. Breathe.'

'I just need my tablets.'

'Can't you go to the doctor here and get a prescription?'

'I broke my insurance,' I admitted.

'You what?'

'My health insurance card,' I explained. 'I used it to jimmy the door open and it broke in two.'

'Smart. So how long does it last?'

'It only took me a minute.'

'No, your "chemical imbalance", I mean.'

'I don't know. I've never tried quitting anything before.'

'What about the black market?'

'What about it?'

'For your pills. We could try the central station in Rome. Train stations are the same everywhere.' Every now and then, Martha would try to sound like she'd spent years on the streets.

'We're not talking about heroin here, Martha,' I said. 'These are perfectly respectable serotonin inhibitors. They don't even get you high. They're not the kind of thing you get on the black market.'

'You can get anything on the black market,' she said in a stiff, tight voice.

'Nah, forget it.'

'Your withdrawal symptoms can't be that bad, then,' she snapped, as if I was putting on an act she'd seen through long ago.

'Tell me, what turned you into such a hard person?' I asked.

'Family planning,' she responded matter-of-factly.

'I really need a coffee. I can hardly see a thing.'

'Well, that's one good thing about Italy. Even the petrol stations sell good coffee.'

'Only there are no petrol stations around here.'

Martha took out her phone and zoomed in on our vicinity. 'You're right. Not one petrol station until Rome. We'll have to drive into the next town. Five kilometres. It even has a palace on a mountain, according to this thing.'

'All I want is coffee. No palaces. Coffee.'

Martha watched me with fear in her eyes as I swerved, with a violence that caught me by surprise too, into the exit to the town.

We followed the sat nav's mad left-right ramblings through the city. Strange how such a monotonous voice can issue the most ludicrous commands. The streets kept getting narrower, and, to my dismay, steeper too. I could feel the walls of the buildings before I saw them. All I wanted to do was to give up, to simply stop driving, but there was someone behind us, there was always someone right behind us. In the warren of one-way streets, turning around wasn't an option. Martha looked at her phone helplessly.

'Nearly there,' she said.

That old chestnut. Whenever you hear it, you can be damn sure catastrophe isn't far behind. It's pretty much the same as 'One last job and then I'll quit.'

We obediently followed the road, which was now falling sharply downhill.

'Just another two hundred metres,' Martha said, but we weren't going to make it: a barricade appeared in the middle of a twist in the road and we braked. The car was now jammed, the handbrake engaged, in a dead-end street on a thirty per cent incline. We had just one question: What now? To which there was unfortunately only one answer: Back. But back is easier said than done, back is actually one of life's most difficult manoeuvres. My skills were un-derdeveloped when it came to going backwards. Reverse was not my favourite gear, and it certainly wasn't made for slopes like this.

Deep breath, put the car into gear, release the handbrake, hit the accelerator.

The engine screeched, then fell suddenly and permanently si-lent. We slid noiselessly down the hill. Just a few seconds, just a few metres, just a wall and a bang. The airbags exploded in our faces, the horn blasted, smoke curled upwards. I was gob-smacked. What I'd just done was of unparalleled stupidity. The fumes ripped open my throat and burned my eyes. I looked at Martha.

'Get out of the car!' someone shouted outside.

I heard Martha moan, saw how slow her movements were as we extracted ourselves from the airbags and opened the doors. Outside, a stunned little crowd were waving their hands about and shouting, 'La macchina!'

Martha was as white as the smoke billowing from the car. Her face and arms were cut and she was coughing. It's not the accident that kills you but the built-in safety features.

'You've wrecked Kurt's car,' she said.

The left headlight was broken and there was a fine crack in the windscreen and a dent in the bonnet. I couldn't understand why the car was making such a fuss: the alarm was still wailing.

'It's a sign, a really bad one!'

'Don't start on about signs now! Next time you can take the train!'

'You killed him!' Martha was clearly in a state of shock, but sadly I wasn't in any kind of altered state, just mildly irritated at my own idiocy. All I'd wanted was a coffee.

A man with his shirt unbuttoned all the way down the front handed Martha a bottle of water, walked over to the smoking car and removed the key, whereupon everything fell silent. Dripping with condescension, he handed me the car key with a shake of the head.

'Dónde cappuccino?' I asked him, and his head jerked towards the barricaded street on the right.

I dragged Martha away by the arm as our audience looked on. The only word I understood was 'la macchina', and that was probably for the best.

'What did you say to him?' Martha asked.

'I asked him where we can get a cappuccino,' I said. 'Where cappuccino? In Spanish. I can still dig up the odd scrap.'

'You want a cappuccino? Now?' Staggering along behind me, Martha looked skewed from her eyes all the way down to her feet. All sense of orientation had deserted her.

'I've been craving a coffee for hours now,' I said. 'But we keep getting side-tracked.'

Ahead of us was a quiet market square, and in it a fountain with no water, a ball with no children and a priest with no parishioners. There were also three closed restaurants and a crowded bar. I came back outside with two cappuccinos and two shots of schnapps and returned to Martha, who was slumped on a kerb.

At last, I thought as I took my first sip, peace at last. We're rid of the banger at last, no more pointless driving around, it's all over at last.

This was only partially true, of course. Nothing was over, plus we looked like tramps, sticky, scratched and wearing the same clothes we'd had on for days. I gulped down the schnapps and put the glass back on the tray.

'Do you think the car will still run?' Martha asked, one eye filling with tears.

'Theoretically,' I replied. Martha nodded.

'So can we drive it or not?'

'The beeping is a problem,' I said. 'We'd be an alarm on wheels. And the airbags would be stuck in our faces the whole time.'

'We can cut them out.'

'And I imagine the seatbelts don't work any more,' I added.

'We don't need them.'

'And then there's the windscreen. And the brakes. And the headlights.'

'Christ, what an absolute shitshow. How could we let something like this happen?'

It was one of those questions there was no point in trying to answer now, after the fact.

The man with the unbuttoned shirt strolled across the square. He passed us with a slight tip of the head and went into the bar.

Two minutes later, incredulous guffaws erupted inside. Guffaws followed by: 'La macchina!' I knew I would hear this word in my sleep and wake up to a pillow exploding in my face.

'What are we going to do?' Martha asked. She must have been utterly desperate if she was still putting me in charge.

'It's Sunday,' I said after a while. 'So we won't find anyone to tow the car.'

'I'm not spending the night here! It's out of the question.'

She scratched frantically at the grazes on her arms. We were sitting in this market square like a couple of kids in a sandpit, except that there were two empty schnapps glasses in front of us and no one was going to pick us up and take us home.

'Of course we can't stay,' I said. 'I say we get out of here, do an Irish goodbye.'

'We can't just leave the car behind.'

'The car was a write-off before this happened. The family will get rid of it. The Italians love a bit of waste disposal.'

'The Irish, the Italians – you're not very politically correct.' She raised her head and looked at me. 'All right then. Let's do a runner.'

We made a wide arc around the square, past new buildings made of cheap concrete, and crossed the main street, where the petrol station was waiting like a bad joke. It was shut.

We sneaked up alleys and back down them again, and a quarter of an hour later, we approached the car from the rear. The interior was still filled with fumes, the slack airbags dangling over the seats. We reached into the back seat and grabbed the little luggage we had, overnight bags stinking of sweat and smoke. It all felt so pointless right then. Martha hunkered down to unscrew the number plate.

'A souvenir,' she said. And for our own safety, I thought. It's best not to leave your address on an illegal scrapheap. Everyone had seen us but nobody knew who we were.

I found myself wanting to go on the run for real. Maybe it was time for a proper crime. I liked the idea of being on a most-wanted list. Unlike Martha, who was now using a towel to wipe down the doors and steering wheel, which I found a bit unnecessary.

'No traces,' she said, 'no problems.'

I looked up at the windows surrounding us. I couldn't see any faces behind the curtains; it was all still. We slunk through the empty streets, past abandoned construction sites, closed restaurants and a bleak playground, and once again Italy was uglier than its reputation would have us believe.

For the first time in years, Martha put her arm around my waist. I couldn't remember the last time we'd walked down the street like this. Maybe it was when we were in our early twenties, when we still believed we could marry each other if the worst came to the worst, sometime in a distant future we never really thought we'd reach. Out of the corner of my eye, I saw she was smiling, in spite of everything. I gave her a kiss on the cheek.

'You're not coming with me, are you?' she asked.

I shook my head.

That afternoon, we were stranded somewhere between partings and passings, between memories and fresh hope. It was time to go our separate ways now. I'd go to an island, and Martha would spend her last few days with Kurt the way they deserved to, true to their ideas of happiness and belonging. I was sure I saw something lighting up within her, a faith she had abandoned long ago but at that moment was almost palpable: a fleeting trust that everything does have meaning after all.

With the number plate under Martha's arm, we waited at the stop for the bus to Rome.

A Farewell to Fathers

Italy hadn't brought me what I'd call happiness. But then, I hadn't expected it to. Very few people achieve happiness in Italy; the country is too full of foreigners looking for it. Germans certainly don't find happiness in Italy, just holiday homes.

I now found myself on a virtually empty ferry sailing across the South Aegean. There are certain journeys where you don't need company, journeys that take place so deep within that the only person you might bump into is yourself.

For the first time in ages, I was travelling without an assignment, without some job or other to keep me going. As there'd been no sailings for a few days, I'd bummed around Athens, a city that had become synonymous with crisis, an entire country now always accompanied by the word 'crisis'. I'd walked down deserted shopping streets, stood in front of the parliament, observed the ghostly quiet of Syntagma Square, visited the occupied university building, sat in cafés, listened to people's stories. I'd sent articles and proposals to editors because my money was running out, but nobody replied. You can be too late for a crisis, like everything else.

At the port, I'd stepped over sleeping bags and onto a ferry that no one else boarded, no one else was allowed to board. Most people got no further than Piraeus. For the refugees stranded here, the sea had long stopped holding the promise of freedom.

It was two in the morning, an eight-hour voyage across the Aegean lay behind me and I had no idea what the island I was now arriving at looked like. You could call what I was doing absurd, the result of too much time and too much despair. I'd reached an age where my understanding of things was diminishing, my life degenerating into a running gag, or what some call trauma: the same experiences kept recurring but with a changing cast, different backdrops. I was still consumed with abandonment, with broken relationships and relationships I hadn't dared start, with loneliness, with me myself. I felt ridiculous and thought that if I went back to the very first loss, if I returned to this founding memory, or at least uncovered a few traces of it, I could lift it, like a curse. The least I hoped for was an exorcism.

We docked, the gangway opened, a piped tune sounded from the loudspeakers and I stood at the bow thinking about the pearly gates I didn't believe in. The promise of a fresh start unfolded before me. It was only an island but I leapt onto it as if bounding across an abyss, that is to say, I stumbled off the ship with all the pathos I could muster.

The dimly lit pier was deserted except for two men leaning on their cars and holding up signs. They looked like sons who'd given up their own lives long ago to continue what their fathers had left behind. One of them, a muscle-bound poseur, yelled the name of his guesthouse at me and bragged about the 'sea view and breakfast'. The other man, a forlorn figure who'd obviously just dragged himself out of either his bed or a bar, was staring at the sea and puffing on a roll-up. Needless to say, I opted for him. He threw my bag into the boot and took one more look around, but I was still the only tourist who'd got off the ferry that April night.

Everything in the small, grubby car seemed to clatter and quake as we drove through the gloom. I saw no houses, no mountains, no beach; I trusted him blindly. I was a nameless foreigner travelling light. Nobody knew anything about me and nobody was interested. I'd always loved how you can vanish when you travel alone. In fact, the possibility of dropping off the radar was probably the main appeal. Maybe I'd inherited this too, from someone I was never related to.

His name was Yannis, the driver said, and that was all he said. None of the usual questions: where was I from, how long was I staying. I wouldn't have had answers anyway. I was here searching for something, everything else I'd already forgotten. Martha and Kurt and Italy were far away now. Yannis woozily navigated the twists in the road. I could smell the booze on his breath, the scent of aniseed wafting through the car. After a sharp left turn, he parked the car and we got out. Little lights marking a path through an unkempt garden, a white house with a blue wooden door and a terrace facing the sea, which I could hear but not see. Everything ahead of me was black, not even a glimpse of the moon.

**

When I opened the shutters the next morning, I was unprepared for the beauty of the cliffs and the sea. There was something unreal about the view, too perfect, like it had been photoshopped. I'd never woken up to anything like this before. I was used to waking up in cities because I thought I needed them. Nature was a stranger to me. I didn't understand it, I loathed tranquillity. I'd always been the kind of person who avoids trips to the countryside and skips over scenery descriptions in books, and now here I was. Yannis brought me Turkish coffee on the terrace and immediately left again.

As I looked out at the view, my mind emptied. One after another, my thoughts dissolved, until only one remained: this would be a good place to disappear, maybe even a good place to die. Ernesto had known that. He must have been happy here, and maybe that really was the most important thing. I hoped I could make it the most important thing to me, at least. If nothing else, I wanted the people who'd left me to have found happiness.

I gazed at the sea, and it was all-embracing, it all embraced me, and I thanked the man who'd walked out for luring me here.

A message from beyond, and I'd listened. I smiled, barely able to believe I was thinking such nonsense, but I was. At that moment, I was both the thought and the laughing-at-the-thought, the precocious little kid and the greying woman.

I sat for hours with the sun on my face until Yannis placed a grilled fish on the table and said, 'Hungry?'

Maybe it was because the season hadn't started yet, because there wasn't exactly much going on here, but also maybe because I was alone, because the folk here looked out for people who were alone, and when those people were women folk looked out for them even more. He'd just moved here last summer, Yannis said. Before that, he'd studied physics in London, but now his parents needed him here. We sat together on the terrace looking across the bay, the sky light blue, the cliffs dark green, the sea turquoise, the smell of oregano, thyme and lavender in the air. We smoked in silence.

'My life's been so much better since I came here,' Yannis said after a while. 'I didn't like London.'

I considered the possibility of running a B&B on the island, making jam, pressing olive oil, and then I briefly considered the possibility of falling in love. Very briefly, obviously.

***

I put on my shoes and set off, away from the bay, up the hills, not knowing where to look or what exactly I was looking for, just a fuzzy assumption that there must be traces of him somewhere. Ernesto had left nothing behind in our flat but the T-shirt he'd slept in the previous night. For years afterwards, I'd kept it hidden in the drawer under my bed and would secretly wear it every now and then, a dark-blue T-shirt that went down to my knees and smelled of aftershave. I threw it out long after it had stopped smelling of him, when we were moving into yet another new life, into my mother's next marriage. I didn't keep a scrap of it.

I'd waited for years and was finally forced to accept that people could vanish from my life without anything or anyone being held responsible.

Thirty years later, and I was looking for a sign of him in a faraway idyll. What did I expect to find? A dark-blue T-shirt hanging from a branch? I kept walking, leaving the path to trek along donkey trails, encountering nobody. In the distance I could see on one side a white village, on the other cliffs jutting out into the sea. My legs were getting weak; I hadn't even thought to bring water. Keep walking, don't fall. I was unfit but tough. I'd been in this condition for years, and I was regularly astounded by how far I could get when I was on my last reserves of energy. My last reserves of energy seemed to have boundless potential.

Why had he come to this island? Why had he hidden away from what most people consider the world? What was all that crap about picking a fight with the wrong family? What had the policeman in Bellegra meant? Did they really think he was mixed up with the mafia? It was preposterous.

So he idolised Al Capone. But people who idolise Al Capone are really just into the films, Scorsese. Yes, he was a trombonist, and he used to head out to work in the evening with a trombone case that could potentially hold any manner of firearm. And okay, a couple of times I saw wads of cash in the case where his trombone should've been, but I never saw a gun. Ernesto was a gambler. He used to spend his nights in casinos, and I suppose he had the odd win. That's the thing about gambling, everyone wins at some point. The money was always gone the next day. I assume my mother never saw a single note.

And it's true he'd go AWOL from time to time, prompting my mother to go on drinking binges in the kitchen. It was her way of going insane with jealousy. Her way of fighting for her man involved large amounts of self-pity. She suffered so fiercely she thought no one would dare leave her, that they'd be afraid she wouldn't survive it.

I imagined myself saying to her back then: Don't worry Mum, he's away on mafia business. She probably would've been relieved. Better a guy who sent people to sleep with the fishes than a guy who slept with other women. Anyway, she would've happily gone to prison for him. She was that kind of woman, the kind who loves with every fibre of her being, as she liked to say, and without an ounce of sense, as I often thought. She thought she was romantic and I thought she was naïve. But what child tells her mother she's naïve? It rarely happens while the child is still a child.

Leaving aside his trombone case, his wads of cash and his secrets, I couldn't imagine Ernesto being a criminal for one important reason: he was a coward. I recalled an incident I hadn't thought about in thirty years, an incident I'd forgotten because I'd wanted to forget it. We were on our way home after he picked me up from school one day. I must have been about six or seven and my hair was almost black, like his. The area we lived in wasn't the best. Our flat was on a main road in the seedy part of town, five minutes from the motorway and red-light district, where the losers, immigrants and Nazis lived. Today you'd say it was disadvantaged. Back then, it was best to say nothing at all.

They were standing in our way, a pack of teenage boys, a barricade.

Combat boots, bomber jackets, shaved heads, the usual getup. They called us dagos, told us to fuck off back to where we came from and spat in our faces, first him, then me. Ernesto just hung his head and held my hand. That's all he did, hold my hand while six Nazis took it in turns to spit in my face. Next time they'd kill us, they said, and trooped off. We continued on our way without exchanging a word. When we reached our building, Ernesto let go of my hand and laid into a rubbish bin, started punching it, kicking it. It was a metal bin, so he created more noise than damage. He beat the thing up for minutes on end. I stood a few metres away, smiling and shrugging whenever someone passed who didn't seem to consider this normal behaviour. I kept a lookout while he took his rage out on the rubbish. When he was through, we went home and had homemade pasta for lunch.

Maybe he just wanted to keep out of trouble. Who needs trouble when they're already involved with the mafia? I could twist and turn things whichever way I pleased. My memories were malleable: I could do with them whatever I wanted.

***

The countryside provided no clues. All I saw was meadows in bloom and a capsized sailing boat rotting in the bay. Nothing stirred in the single village I came to, apart from a few cats skittering about. I'd been wandering without purpose or point, encountering nothing but my own memories and a growing sense of eeriness. Now, I'm not one of those people who intuits things. I can't be doing with woo-woo bullshit about having a sixth sense. I see what I see, hear what I hear, and this categorically does not involve spirits, supernatural forces, premonitions, revenants and the like. I can't even stand astrology. But there was something eerie about this island. This was the last straw for me: the thought that there might be some kind of connection here, that I was *intuiting* a connection with something or someone, that not only was I slipping into a midlife crisis but I might also be acquiring spiritual tendencies. Maybe it had something to do with stopping the antidepressants, one of the loose ends in the ball of undesirable side effects. It wasn't like a filter had disappeared and been replaced by clear-headedness, raw perception. No, what had arrived instead was esotericism. The worst possible perception of reality.

I walked along the seafront and decided on the third taverna I passed. It's a universal principle: if you want to get to know a place, find where the locals drinks. It had low music and faded awnings, a low-profile kind of place. I sat down at one of the many empty tables outside, and when the barman came and I ordered a beer, he told me they only had Mythos this week, which I liked the sound of, even though he warned me it was the worst beer in Greece. The bad mood seemed to be part of his character, and I liked that too.

In front of me on the table lay a tidy heap of empty husks, the sunflower seed hulls often left behind by men who are on diets, experiencing withdrawal symptoms or suffering from some other psychological defect. I've never met anyone who eats sunflower seeds because they like them. There is no clearer sign of nervousness and neurosis than the constant munching of seeds. I brushed them aside and replaced them with an ashtray.

I sat there until dark, drinking, smoking, staring at the sea and waiting for something to happen.

The next day, I did the same. Brushed the husks off the table, drank and waited. By now, chasing after answers seemed pointless; the harder I looked, the more elusive they became.

By the third day I was part of the furniture, allowed, indeed obliged, to fetch my beer from the fridge myself. Within a week at most, there'd be something going on between me and the barman, whatever that something was and whether or not I was aware of it. As the only unaccompanied female tourist here under sixty, men and rumours were sure to follow me around like stray cats.

Later I sat at the bar with six Greeks in tracksuit bottoms, all of us drinking Mythos, which really was vile, and talking in low voices. Greece is a melancholy country, they said, where people rarely laugh out loud. The barman told me the others' backstories. I learned that the potter's husband had died the previous year. I found out that the mother of the bloke sitting at the end of the bar on the right pressed her own olive oil, and that I could buy little plastic bottles of it from him (under the counter, naturally). I heard the story behind the little memorial stone at the crossroads (a traffic accident a few years ago) and about how the family coped afterwards (not well). The brother of the man sitting at the far left of the bar had killed himself in Athens. He'd worked for a bank but had been a decent man nonetheless. No one wanted to understand it.

They talked about pressure, about how the male suicide rate had shot up since the crisis started. Others said that the shock had passed, that crisis was now the norm. Whether it would ever stop, whether things would get better, nobody knew, nor did they care any more. The men said they wanted the drachma back and showed me the currency. They all carried old banknotes in their pockets and there was a thousand drachma bill tucked behind the spirit bottles.

'Fuck the EU,' they said. For months they'd only been allowed to withdraw sixty euros a day. They all had two or three accounts with different banks now but there were no transactions being done any more, it was impossible to transfer money abroad. I'd been running a tab for days, working up a bill high enough for my large denominations. Solidarity had never been easier: all I had to do was blow my money on this Greek island.

The taverna owner was sitting alone at his table, an old man doubled over with stomach pain. He told us he'd taken a volume of Dylan Thomas down from the shelf the day before, because Dylan Thomas can ease all kinds of pain, and inside it he'd found an envelope containing 100,000 drachmas. His rainy-day fund. He burst out laughing, which made his stomach hurt even more. His emergency reserves were now just a bookmark. He no longer cared whether his patrons paid today, tomorrow or never. When he locked up every evening, he left the ouzo out front for the hardest drinkers. The hardest of all were the Swedes, who slept on the chairs outside. People came here from all over Europe to crash and burn. You could buy wine here by the kilo: half a kilo for €2.80. If it was self-obliteration you were after, there was nowhere cheaper, plus you had a view of the sea thrown in for no extra charge. The poor Swedes, I thought, having to leave home to drink themselves to death.

The barman poured us rakomelo, an anise brandy heated up with cinnamon. It was a cold night and the Greeks in their tracksuit bottoms told me about the hard winters, about summers in which they did nothing but work, about alcohol that had stopped helping long ago. We drank to the taverna owner and to the good news that the boat with his false teeth on board had finally arrived. He could smile again, and tomorrow there'd be shark for dinner.

No one mentioned Ernesto and I didn't dare ask about him. The braying of a donkey filled the silence, a shrieking sound I'd never heard before, and when I asked whether they were shrieks of lust or pain, the men shook their heads, unable to see the difference.

***

'Get in,' Yannis said. 'I'll show you paradise.' He was leaning against his car as I walked out onto the terrace. In comparison to our first meeting, he looked fresh-faced, almost young, and maybe he actually was young. It was hard to tell. He had no hair and no front-left incisor. Not much in the way of brains either, according to the barman. *Stupidito.* I imagine the barman thought that any man who liked me must be an idiot. He was the only one on the island with a brain in his head, an Albanian who thought the Greeks were a bunch of layabouts. Yannis was a communist too, he'd said, and I readily believed it. There was a whiff of the hippy about him, which made him either suspicious or just pathetic in the eyes of the others. Allegedly he grew his own weed somewhere around the house, walked barefoot down country lanes and imbibed homeopathic tinctures prepared by his friend, who was also called Yannis. His parents had moved here from Athens a few years back. His father had built the house that was now the B&B, and the rest of the family were stuck in rooms without a view. I'd heard about all of this, and they were all good reasons to get in his car.

We tore along the winding roads, Elvis playing in the background as Yannis told me about the time he'd managed to drive to the port, a journey that usually takes twenty minutes, in twelve minutes. His friends, who had to catch the six o'clock sailing, had got out of the car and puked into the sea. But they made their ferry. He laughed, and I noticed there was more than one tooth missing. As we drove further north, he pointed out the most authentic tavernas, the scuzziest cafés, the most breathtaking bays. We visited a monastery hewn into the rocks, drank their homemade herb liqueur and joked with the monks. They told stories, sang and slapped their habits with amusement at everything Yannis said. I'd never seen monks laughing before but I suppose they were drunk too. This island was a paradise full of pissheads, a place where people lived slower and died quicker.

Yannis took the curves without taking his foot off the pedal. I let him do it, because he could. I closed my eyes. Sometimes trust is your only option. When I reopened them, he pointed to an isolated house far removed from the road and said, 'If you ever kill someone back home, you can hide out there, no one will ever find you. I'll take care of you.'

It was genuinely one of the most romantic, most reassuring things anyone had ever said to me. In this life, there's not a single catastrophe we can rule out. From the moment we're born, we're capable of anything. In this life, you need someone who will help you make your getaway, no matter how safe things may seem right now.

'Rumour has it some Italians hid out there once,' Yannis said.

I tried to sound casual as I said I'd like to go see it, but my voice came out shrill.

'It's a ruin,' said Yannis. 'There's nothing to see.'

'But I need to know where you plan to hide me,' I responded. 'I might not kill anyone if the house is a dump.'

'I've never been in it. Bad things happened there.'

'What kind of things?'

'We'd best keep away.'

'I want to see it. Please.'

'You're not right in the head. We've spent hours driving through paradise and the only thing you're interested in is some tumbledown house.'

A house that had already disappeared behind a bend. We were getting further and further away from it.

'Stop the fucking car!'

Startled, Yannis slammed down on the brake and gaped at me.

'This isn't normal,' he said as he turned the car around.

'Thanks,' I muttered.

We turned off the road and drove up a narrow, bumpy track. Even from a distance, I could see there was no front door, the windows were like dead eyes and there was nothing surrounding the house but weeds and scorched earth.

'What are we doing here?' Yannis asked, not expecting an answer. I knew I'd disappointed him by turning my back on his paradise. We weren't in any kind of relationship, yet we were already having our first crisis. But if I thought he was annoyed or insulted, I was wrong; he wasn't. He was scared. He pulled up in front of the house and lit two cigarettes for us.

'We'll go in after this,' he said.

He told me a crime had been committed here years before he arrived. There were even rumours about the mafia, he said, shaking his head.

'You know,' he said, 'there's no crime here. We screw each other over, sure, but we don't kill each other. We don't even steal each other's wives. If that kind of thing starts happening, we'll all lose in the end. There's nowhere for us to go. An island like this is a prison. If you fuck up, there's nowhere to run.'

I didn't look at Yannis, just kept staring at the house, at the bricks; I was sure I could make out bullet holes.

'What are we doing here?' he asked again.

'Just looking,' I said, and when he refused to believe me, I said I was a crime writer. Or at least planning to become one. The Germans are mad for crime, I said, and a crime novel, maybe even a whole crime series based on the Greek islands, would make me stinking rich. As I was talking, I began to believe what I was saying. I promised him he'd be in it, and that when I was rich, I'd come back with bags of money, all of it for him, as I'd already have enough for myself. All he had to do now was get out of the car with me, all he had to do was tell me what he knew; but he didn't know much. Nobody talked about what had happened here.

We walked towards the house slowly, not because we thought we were in danger, not because we feared for our lives, but because we were afraid of one thing: that there could be a corpse in there. We all fantasise about running into our first love and our first crushing disappointment, but we seldom fantasise about them being in a state of decomposition.

Yannis looked in the windows while I stepped warily into the house.

No bodies, no remnants of bodies, no bones. Not even a smell. By the wall there was a bed with no mattress, no bedclothes, just the frame. But what a frame. It was colossal, despotic even: around two square metres of solid steel with a curlicued head-board, decorative spheres on all four posts and a wrought steel roof. A canopy bed with curtains hanging in tatters. I'd expected to feel a lot of things, but instead there was just one thought in my mind: anyone with a bed like that deserves to be shot.

The house consisted of a single room, and the room pretty much consisted of just this bed. By the wall on the right there was a sink, and beside it a gas cylinder. No books, no clothes, no tins of tomatoes. No furniture, no shoes, no letters, no pills and no bottles of wine, not even empty ones. No pens, no paper, no photos. Nothing. Just dust and grime. And this bed, which couldn't have been Ernesto's. He'd never been here, there'd been a mix-up. Dead people are easily mistaken for each other. Desires even more so. Behind me I heard Yannis coming in. I turned around and said, 'They've ransacked the place.'

He took just one look at the room and said that something wasn't right. Namely the bed. There were many things about the bed that weren't right, but one that was particularly striking: it was valuable.

'That's stainless steel,' Yannis said after inspecting it up close. 'It's ugly, a nightmare, pure porn, but it's stainless steel. No one ransacks a house and leaves the metal behind. People are ripping heating pipes out of houses these days because metal prices are high. This place hasn't been ransacked. Someone cleared out their stuff. And whatever they couldn't carry, they left behind.'

I started to feel weirdly cold in this house. I was freezing from the inside out. I never knew there could be such coldness inside me. I turned to go, I just wanted to get out of there, and I'd already reached the door when I spotted them. In the corner, to the right of the door frame: sunflower seed husks. In a tidy heap, just like the ones I'd been brushing off the table over the past few days.

Someone had sat in this corner, waiting. Someone had sat here, nearly dying from the tension.

We walked to the car without looking back once, and Yannis said it wasn't a bad idea, the crime writing. Elvis blared from the car stereo, Yannis raced around the twists in the road, and the world was exactly the same as it had been before, on the way, and yet it felt further off. A connection had been broken, a connection to my own past. Anyone who's been walked out on wants one final conversation, some final clarity, an admission that it had been a mistake to separate. This hope had never faded for me, not even after Ernesto died. But the thought that

he mightn't have died at all, that he hadn't got in touch despite
still being alive, robbed me of the strength that had allowed me
to forgive him up to now. There might be a truth that would
bring all my survival mechanisms crashing down. It could quite
possibly drive me over the edge. But as yet I'd seen nothing, just
a heap of seeds.

'Hey,' I heard Yannis say beside me. 'Still there?'

'No,' I replied.

'I was asking whether you like pig.'

'Pigs?'

'Yes. You know, the cute, fat animal? Pot-roasted, with potatoes, tomatoes, thyme, rosemary.'

When you don't know anything any more but have a nagging
suspicion, when you've absolutely no idea what's going to happen next, what else can you do but pull up a chair and eat roast
pork?

Yannis served dinner on the terrace. As I barely uttered a word
and we didn't know each other nearly well enough to eat in silence, he talked and I nodded. Around us, night began to fall.

A boatload of refugees had arrived in the bay that morning,
he said. The first thing the refugees saw was a drunken Swede.
The second thing they saw was the water and food the villagers
had brought. The third was a policeman, the only one on the island, who put them on a bus and drove them to the port, where
the next day the ferry would leave for Piraeus. As Yannis shook
his head, an expression of utter helplessness on his face, the sky
darkened. Within seconds, the village ahead of us had disappeared, thunder was shaking the cliffs, lightning illuminating
the bay. It was a diabolical scene. What was being unleashed was
naked, brute rage. Zeus was well within the realms of possibility;
I was sure I could see his spear. Then everything went dark. All
the lights had gone out, the village extinguished. We turned on
the torches on our phones and carried our dishes inside.

Yannis was either groaning or cursing. Given that I knew his language even less well than I knew him, it was hard to tell the difference. The alarm was beeping again, the snooze button having already been hit several times. He had to make breakfast, he said. No need, I said, I was fine. He just laughed, got dressed and made eggs for the apartment upstairs while I went back to sleep.

Yannis came back without a tray, shaved his testicles for reasons unclear to me, and crawled back into bed. The shutters were closed, the air conditioning was running and a cockerel crowed every hour. I'd no idea how long I'd slept for. It must have been the deepest sleep I'd had in months.

When I asked him if I could borrow his car, just for the afternoon, he shook his head as if to say: Go ahead, do what you like.

'The key is in my trouser pocket,' he said. Then he burrowed under the cover and I set off.

***

I stood alone in front of the ruin, the sea rumbling behind me. I walked around the house, trod across the little plot of land surrounding it, peeked into the little privy and quickly withdrew again. Finally, I entered the room, sat down on the floor and rubbed the seeds between my fingers. They were a few weeks old at most. If it was Ernesto, if he was still alive, he must have sat in this corner many times. Underneath the husks, I discovered a dark stain. Possibly blood. I'd only seen Ernesto bleed once. It was a Sunday. He'd been practising the trombone in the living room when my mother started screaming at him. He kept right on playing, ignoring the insults, blowing harder and harder into the instrument until finally she grabbed it from him, drew back her arm and rammed the trombone back between his teeth. His lip split and blood ran down his chin. I remember sitting on the floor and continuing with my puzzle as if they weren't there. I never found out what the row was about.

And now here I was again, sitting in a corner, trying to fit together pieces of a puzzle, waiting for a picture to form. I'd catch him, the man who sat at my table chewing seeds, always disappearing just before I arrived. The man who was literally spitting his message out in front of me.

I scanned the room one last time, did one more lap of this abandoned secret, walked out through the open door and made my way through the weeds towards the brambles. It lay right in front of me, a grey cloth encrusted with earth, just the corner of a grip sticking out, like a hastily wrapped gift. I propped myself up with one hand and used the other to dig the pistol out of the ground. Why had someone buried a gun? How long had it been here? Had it been deliberately left, or had it somehow been mislaid and then buried by the wind? The questions swirled, but nothing could surprise me at this point. It was too late for surprises. I'd accepted that I had no control over anything any more.

The gun felt heavy in my hand. I removed it from the cloth, pulled back the barrel and saw that it was loaded. I didn't know much about firearms, but I knew enough to fire one. I'd visited a shooting range once years ago, at an old US army training centre deep in West Berlin. They'd told me about guns, how to handle them, the laws, the safety precautions, the various calibres, and I'd forgotten all of it except for one thing: how much fun it is to shoot. I aimed at the house, supported my right hand with my left one, focused on a point below the window, looked through the iron sights and fired. The bang left me momentarily deaf, but the recoil gave me a warm feeling. What was flowing through me, of course, was pure power. I remembered how long it had stayed with me before. Hours after I'd left the shooting range, I was still feeling invincible. It had been a long time since I'd walked through the streets with my head so high. I strode back to the car now in exactly the same way, except that this time, I still had the weapon in my hand.

***

The barman was cycling up and down the street. I suspected it was the first bike he'd owned since he was a kid, brand new, the words *Orient Comfort* emblazoned across the frame. I say cycling, but it was more like parading. He was the village cockerel on a red bike. His skin was surprisingly soft, the potter had whispered to me. His name was Grigori.

I sat down at my usual table, which was unoccupied and not yet covered in seeds. It was early afternoon, the holidaymakers were on their first Mythos and lonely retired women were arranging to meet up for dance meditation. I just waited. I knew it wouldn't be long before someone came along to either flirt or moan, which to me were one and the same. People always started with one and finished with the other.

He'd been here for seventeen years, Grigori said after he joined me. For fifteen years now he'd been working in the same bar. It could be his if he wanted, but he'd had enough. This was his last summer, he said. He'd be gone before the last tourists had left the island.

'The women are gone,' he said. 'The money too. Greece is no good any more. There's nothing here apart from the sun. Nothing's being planned, nothing's being built, nothing's being paid for. I'm tired.' He'd been saying that for days – years, probably. 'I haven't been swimming once, no time,' he said, gazing at the sea as if it was his ex-wife.

From the kitchen, we heard the sound of something slithery slapping against the worktop, followed by cursing. Someone was tenderising an octopus. A young Pakistani man came out and tossed his apron at Grigori.

'You know who's even lazier than the Greeks?' Grigori said. 'The Pakistanis!'

With that, he went inside and I had new company. It was impossible to be alone here. The constant presence of others was making me nervous. I wasn't managing to disappear here, I stuck out like a sore thumb. Nobody wants people around when they're trying to find themselves.

The Pakistani man showed me a photo on his phone of a massive joint.

'You smoke?'

'No,' I said. 'I don't.'

No one had ever believed me when I said this before, and he didn't believe me either. He winked at me moronically, but at his age, it was just about forgivable. He can't have been more than twenty-three.

'You big, I'm small,' he said. 'No problem for me.' He showed me photos of a woman who looked a few years older than me. He'd slept with her. 'No problem. You big, I'm small.'

I'm not sure whether it was this sentence or a surge of misplaced maternal instinct, but I suddenly felt an urge to phone my mother.

'I need to make a call,' I said. Never before had the thought of my mother made me want to call her, I realised. It had always been a matter of politeness, that nagging 'I really ought to get in touch' feeling. Now I found myself frantically scrolling through my phone for her name: *Karin*.

She answered right away, with the familiar exaggerated delight that immediately made me want to hang up.

'My daughter!' she cried into the phone.

'Yes,' I said. 'It is she.'

'Lovely to hear from you!'

'Yes.'

'I've been thinking about you.'

'I know.'

'But I suppose not hearing from you is a good sign, right?'
'Oh yes, it's all good.'
'That's what I thought. My daughter is doing well, too well!'
'I'm in Greece at the moment …'
'I won't keep you in that case. This must be costing you a fortune.'
'It doesn't cost a fortune, Karin, they got rid of roaming charges in Europe. It costs the same as at home.'
'You're always so clued in.'
'You know, I've been thinking a lot about Ernesto lately.'
'Ernesto? Why?'
'Didn't he use to say he'd like to visit Greece?'
'Greece? No, he was never interested in Greece. It was me who wanted to go. I wanted to take a holiday in Crete, just once. But where did we go instead? Denmark. No, Ernesto never wanted to go anywhere, at least not with me. He was on the road so much with his job, I suppose. Don't you remember?'

I remembered everything, or at least everything I could have known about at the time. I asked her if it was really true that she'd never heard from him again, and she asked me why I wanted to know now, why I was reopening old wounds. I should take a leaf out of her book and forget him, she said.

'Ernesto. It's a long time ago now,' she said. 'I haven't thought about him in ages.'

My mother, a champion forgetter. She was a happy woman, I was sure. She was able to repress everything, forget snubs, rejections and failures and start afresh as if she'd never been hurt by love. She loved with inexhaustible innocence and naivety, over and over again. I couldn't remember her ever taking a break. She layered happiness on top of unhappiness, unhappiness on top of happiness, at such speed and in such volumes that she herself was buried beneath it all. 'He's dead ten years now,' I said.

'You see? An eternity ago.'

A closed chapter. First he'd left her, then he'd died. It couldn't be more final: for her, the story had ended. My mother's husbands were my mother's husbands. It never occurred to her that to me they'd been fathers, stepfathers, friends, enemies, rapists. Her dependency on men had driven me to absolute independence. My freedom was a curse, and I wanted to at least be able to lay the blame at her door.

'It was never easy with him,' she said. 'I mean an Italian, with me, a northern German. We had some dreadful rows, you can imagine.'

'I was there, Karin. Please don't go on as if I didn't know him.'

'But you were just a child. He was always nice to you, I'll give him that.'

'How come we never visited Italy with him?'

'No money.'

'That was the reason, no money?'

'You only go back when you've made it, he said. Not as a small-time trombonist. Maybe he was ashamed of me too. I don't know. No one ever came to visit us. Such a big family and I never met any of them. Odd really, when I think about it.'

I agreed with her, it was odd, though I'd never questioned it back then. I hadn't missed his family, quite the contrary: his being alone bound him to us. A man as lost as he was would never run away, I'd thought.

'I did meet him again once,' my mother said. 'It must have been shortly after we separated.'

'He came to visit?'

'No,' she said. 'I ran into him.'

'Where?'

'Ikea. I was there with Rainer.'

'Rainer who?'

'Come on, you remember! Rainer.'

'The bald bloke?'

'No. Well, a bit balding at the back maybe.'

'The cokehead?'

'Betty!'

'Rainer. I'd forgotten about him.'

'Yes, well, it didn't last very long. But he did hang our curtains for us.'

'At least they lasted, I suppose.'

'I shouldn't have to listen to this cheek.'

'You don't have to. I wanted to talk about Ernesto.'

'Right,' she said. 'He was there with some woman. Arm in arm, they were.'

'What kind of woman?'

'Another woman, a new one. We didn't talk for long. You know what it's like. What are you supposed to talk about in the middle of Ikea?'

At every new stage of life you end up back at Ikea, where every hope begins and ends, I thought. Where you start over for the umpteenth time and then get yourself a hot dog.

'Did you ever think he might be leading a double life?'

'Is this some kind of interrogation?' She laughed. 'These are weird questions you're asking.'

'Just doing a bit of research.'

'Research for what?'

'For myself. I think about him a lot, you know. I miss him. I've always missed him.'

'I'm sorry, I'm so sorry about everything. If I could go back, I'd ...'

'You'd do it all differently, I know.'

This had always been her get-out-of-jail-free card, and predictably, I heard her start to cry. Whoever cries first is in the right, and, more importantly, you can't have a go at someone who's crying. It was how she got out of every unpleasant discussion, every possible criticism, every uncomfortable question. I wondered how many more years it would take for my rage to get the better of my pity, and whether she'd live to see it happen. I hoped not, for her sake.

'It's fine,' I said, as usual. 'It's fine. I lived to tell the tale.'

She sniffled once more – a bit theatrically, I thought – and told me she loved me, and I apologised. These conversations had become a ritual, albeit one we didn't perform as often as we used to. It was as pointless as it was painful.

After I hung up, the barman put a plate of burnt octopus on the table. 'It's on the house,' he said.

Before me was a pile of hacked-up arms the colour of coal. He brought me a lemon to go with them, and the day descended into anxious despondency. I was surrounded by pissed-up Swedes and herb-gathering yogis. No sign of a father, no sunflower seeds. I waited but he didn't show. It was all so familiar. Everything was repeating itself. My life story was a story of waiting, waiting for someone to return until the day I decided I'd had enough, packed my bags and ran. I sucked at a cold, burnt arm.

The sun went down like it knew nothing of unhappiness. Just because it looked pretty didn't make it romantic. The sun doesn't give a shit about anything. Go ahead, burn away, I thought. Burn shrubs, minds, ambition. Burn sobriety, skin, sadness. Make me look old when there's no shade. Make me squint into the light. And stop telling me I ought to be having fun.

Ahead of me on the beach, hands were thrust towards the sky. It was the same each evening, everyone's camera trained on the setting sun. The lucky ones had someone to position in the foreground; everyone else grew misty-eyed. Another day vanishing into the sea, another day less. They were going by faster and faster. I thought about the gun in my bag and it had a strangely reassuring effect, gave me inner peace, almost. Let others meditate if they want. As darkness fell, the creatures of the night arrived and sat down at my table. Those of us who were alone had seats going spare, and they kept on coming. The ferry had belched them out, a horde of old regulars. Many had been coming here for twenty years. They wouldn't manage another twenty. They were already going downhill and that was their conversation topic for the night. Paradise had lapsed into a geriatric hospital. It didn't take long – people wreck everything, even if it's just by talking. They talked about their illnesses like they'd once talked about music, drugs and affairs, congratulating themselves if their worst affliction was knee trouble. They were leftovers congregated in a good place for a few final happy days. They would die before me. I don't know why that came into my head. I was beginning to fear the loss that was to come. I'd have to find myself younger friends. I chose to be unhealthy because I didn't want to be the last one left. For fear of surviving, I was running myself into the ground, and as I did so, I sat in silence, listening to the motorboats roar away. Children squealed in the distance and the guitarist next to me was too drunk to find a rhythm, any rhythm at all.

***

Yannis cleared my clothes off the sofa in his bedroom. The place had to resemble a reception again by tomorrow, he said. It was only then that I realised that his room belonged to everyone here, and I was suddenly terrified that his parents would wake up. It was a fear I hadn't experienced in a very long time indeed.

We listened to Amy Winehouse on YouTube, and Yannis said he'd bumped into her once in London, a few days before she died, in a stairwell. They'd been on their way to the same dealer.

'It wasn't the drugs that killed her,' he said. 'It was love.' He told me about street battles in Athens, about the months he and his friends had spent rioting. He clicked on videos of tear gas being sprayed and truncheons flying on those nights in Exarcheia. It seemed that every chapter of his life was available on YouTube. I listened and watched, staying with him only because I didn't know what you're supposed to do with someone you're not actually with. Post-coital politeness, you might call it.

Yannis said that the people here used binoculars to spy out of their windows, that gossip was as essential to life here as the sea and ouzo. Most of the men spent their winters alone. Tourism hardens the heart, he said. At the end of their holidays, women pack their suitcases, put on their trousers and shoes, and slip onto the ferry before it gets dark. There was just one taverna, one bar the men could sit at in the evenings, and by December, they'd have nothing left to say to each other. Anyone with the wherewithal left to try their luck on the mainland.

How tired he looked when he said, 'I have to go get my sign.' The sign with the name of his B&B. The sign he held while he waited around for guests he could coax into his car along with their suitcases.

He hated it, he said. He hated that sign. He disappeared behind it, it hid him and everything he was. *Lofkes Studio*, a beautiful house, a fantastic view of the bay, excellent reviews on all platforms, and he himself slept in the back looking out at the courtyard while his parents slept upstairs. *Reception* stuck to his door and no name.

***

I awoke to a distant ringing and rooted through the clothes that had been ripped off and dropped to the floor. Eventually I saw the name *Martha* illuminated on my phone.

'Are you there?' she asked.

'I am now, I couldn't find my phone.'

'No, are you still on the island, I mean.'

'Yes, still here.'

'So, how is it?'

I surveyed pulled blinds, a sleeping man, an ashtray with two stubbed-out joints, my bag, which contained an excavated gun, and my cellulite-riddled naked thigh.

'It's beautiful,' I said. 'Paradise, I guess.'

'Why "I guess?"'

'He's here,' I said. 'He's here eating sunflower seeds.'

'Who?'

'Ernesto. I saw his house, where he used to live. And I saw his seeds.'

'What seeds?'

'He eats sunflower seeds.'

'Sunflower seeds?'

'Yeah, there are husks all over the place. The house, the bar, everywhere.'

'Loads of people do that. When they're quitting smoking, on diets, all that agony, there are always husks everywhere.'

'It's him. Never mind the husks, he's alive.'

'But you haven't actually seen him.'

'No.'

'Are you all right, Betty?'

I glanced at Yannis, who was still asleep. 'Hang on a minute, I'll go outside. I'm not alone.'

'So you're screwing around as well as looking for your dead father?'

'He wasn't my father.'

'You'd do well to remember that,' Martha said. 'To be a little less, I don't know, a little less obsessional.'

Martha was right, of course, I was out of control. It can happen; it was age, hormones, yearning. When it came to my inner life, I'd become a bit of a hypochondriac.

'How's Kurt?' I asked.

'We're taking the ferry tomorrow,' Martha said. 'We're practically en route to you already.'

I was speechless. It wasn't me who'd cracked, it was them. They'd obviously both lost their minds entirely. How he was supposed to survive it was the question.

'It wasn't my idea,' Martha said. 'None of this madness has been my idea. For twenty years he just sat on his sofa, just wanted to be left in peace, and now all of a sudden he seems determined to die in chaos. Keeps going on about how much he loves the sea. Hasn't been anywhere near the sea in decades, mind you, never once mentioned it. If I cork it during the crossing, just throw me overboard, he says, that'd be a good way to go. Let's go and see Betty, he says, let's go to Greece. I swear to God, if I have to listen to one more dying wish ...'

'Can he even walk?' I asked.

'That's the thing,' she said. 'I don't know what Francesca did to him. The woman is a witch. When I arrived at Lake Maggiore, he was sitting in front of the hotel eating tiramisu and drinking liqueur. As if he was on a hard-earned holiday.'

'But that's fantastic,' I said.

'There's nothing fantastic about it!' Martha snapped. 'She's messed with his head, he's taken leave of his senses.'

'Why don't the two of you just stay there?'

'She threw him out.'

'What?'

I'd been ready to believe in it, a final vestige of real love just before the end. For a moment, the romantic ideal had blazed in the distance, only for it to be stamped out now.

'Why did she throw him out?'

'She said she couldn't have him dying in her B&B. Too many have died there already, it'll start to smell fishy, that's how she put it. Not the house itself, but the whole business. One more corpse and I'll end up in prison, she says. Some friend who's in with the police dropped by for an espresso and advised her to get the German out of the house while he's still alive.'

'What the fuck?'

'She's got a screw loose. Sees herself as some kind of angel of death. Honestly, my father has the worst luck with women. You should see it here: every cupboard is crammed with drugs. I don't know what she's running, some kind of amateur hospice. And my father manages to get kicked out. So now it's down to me to take care of him. She gave me a bag of morphine. I don't know how I'm going to get it across the border. At least we're travelling by ferry, I suppose.'

'In his nappy,' I said.

'What do you mean, in his nappy?'

'The drugs, hide them in his nappy.'

'Seriously, Betty. No disrespect to your worldliness, but I'll take care of this myself. I'm not turning my father into a drug mule.'

'But he needs them.'

'I know he needs them, but he doesn't have a prescription. He used up his own medication long ago.'

'Wouldn't it be better to go back to Germany, to a hospital?'

'He doesn't want to, Betty! No way, he said. And I get it, I mean, they can't do anything more for him there. I'd prefer to go to a Greek island with a bag full of morphine too than to a four-bed ward in Hanover.' She groaned. 'I don't know how I'm going to get through this. And every time I wish it was all over, I feel like a monster.'

'We'll get through this together,' I said.

It was false consolation, I knew that. Any time I offered help, it was always in the hope that it would never be needed. My helping skills were sorely lacking, for one simple reason: I was a useless lump with egocentric tendencies. I was sensitive but not caring. My sensitivity applied only to me, and right now I was beyond sensitive, I was overwrought. I was the powder keg upon which I sat and smoked. Whenever I offered help, I quietly feared I would just make things worse. My help was merciless, my advice had led to divorces, chucking-ins of jobs and referrals to psychiatric hospitals. My help was catastrophic. These days, I limited myself to listening, having developed a routine of sorts involving red wine, cake and a shoulder to lean on. But no advice. In practical terms too, I was hopeless. I could barely drive and was incapable of drilling a hole in the wall. Whatever god might be up there, please protect my friends from my help.

'Thanks,' Martha said. 'We arrive tomorrow night.'

'I'll be there,' I said. 'I'll take care of everything.'

***

Someone was whistling 'Azzurro'. I heard it come out of the taverna and make its way towards me. But it was impossible, fate would hardly muck about like that. I sat at my table, defying the storm that had been brewing since morning, looking at the sea, which seemed to be getting more ferocious each day, and holding my breath. Stinking of sweat, 'Azzurro' stopped beside me and placed a beer down in front of me.

It was Grigori the barman. He gave me a nod.

'It's not even midday,' I said. I didn't want to turn into an antisocial alcoholic here, and I knew very well there's just one small step separating a social drinker from an antisocial drinker, and that step is the time of day. Not without reason was I a night owl: it gave me more time for alcohol. What kind of fiend would bring me a beer in the morning?

'You're going to need it,' he said. 'Your friend is inside.'

'What friend?' I asked.

'The sunflower.'

It was the first time I'd seen anything like anger on Grigori's face, real anger.

'If I thought you'd listen, I'd advise you to get out of here. But you're the kind of person who doesn't take advice. I saw it the minute I met you, there's no talking to you. Stubborn as a mule,' he said. Then he went back inside, whistling 'Azzurro' again.

Riveted to the chair, I felt everything – fear, rage, joy, love, hate – and nothing. I took a cautious sip of beer. After thirty years, our first words probably didn't really matter. After such a long separation, it would be impossible to do anything right. Is never better than late, I wondered again. But what was the use of questions, of doubts, now we were only twenty metres apart?

I stood up and went inside.

To the left of the door sat a man, more beard than face, a bag of seeds and a steaming rakomelo on the table in front of him. I'd never thought about how he might look now, how the decades might have changed him. It would have been reasonable to assume that life had ravaged him like it had ravaged everyone else, but instead my picture of him was frozen in time. I'd last seen him when he was forty, as old as I was now, and soon he'd be seventy. Our lives lay in between.

I stood defenceless in the taverna and saw white hair, skin sagging from his body like sadness, and glazed eyes. They remained glazed as he said, 'You haven't changed a bit.'

The sarcasm was new to me, but then everything about him seemed unfamiliar, unrecognisable even. He was sitting there, and it was him and it wasn't him. A scraggy body with a louse-ridden beard, the reek of cheap, sweet cologne, and an arrogance that charged the entire taverna with a cold, tense atmosphere. I felt like lunging at him, I wanted to rip him open and find the person I'd been missing all these decades.

I sat down at his table, unnerved by his inward-looking gaze, a gaze that didn't want to see any more. Finally finding the person I loved only to realise that he'd disappeared within himself, that he'd either lost or killed all the things I'd loved about him – it was unbearable. I knocked back my beer and he took another sip of rakomelo. Where to start, how to begin? I still hadn't uttered a word and I noticed no one else in the place was talking either. The show had begun, silence had descended, but the actors couldn't get their lines out. Meanwhile, the audience ordered their Greek salads.

Ernesto stood up abruptly and motioned for me to follow him.

'Too many ears,' he said.

We sat down at a table outside, the wind blustering around our heads.

'I visited your grave,' I said.

He didn't look at me, just kept staring out at the sea, and asked how I'd found him. He was barely audible in the storm.

'I met your sister,' I said. 'If I understood her correctly, she doesn't send her regards.'

'She's still scared.' Ernesto emptied his glass in one gulp and slammed it down. 'Betty, it's nice to see you, really it is. I never expected to see you again. But what do you want from me?'

'I missed you.' I felt like a fool, running around after the shadow of a non-existent love.

There was no reaction on his sunken face. Instead, I got the same old question of whether I was married. I told him I wasn't.

'Not my fault,' he said, tossing a few husks onto the table.

'Of course not, no one said it was.'

'I've known a lot of German women, Betty. They were all screwed up. Not you, you were just a kid, a sweet little kid. The women, though, they were another story. Off they trot to the doctor every week and they talk and talk and talk, blaming everyone but themselves. And then in the evenings they talk about what they talked about. Mamma mia, can German women moan! And their health insurance pays for it all. What a country!'

He stood up and went back into the taverna.

I wasn't a kid any more when he left us, but then I'd never felt like one when I was around him. Dickhead, I thought. Had I been too young to notice back then, or had he turned into one later? It can happen to the best of men, turning into a dickhead. Sometimes it happens the morning after the night before.

He returned with two bottles of beer and two ouzos. He put one beer down in front of me and set the other drinks down for himself. His eyes were clearing. Ernesto obviously needed a few drinks to wake up in the morning.

'I only drink on Saturdays,' he said. 'And today is Saturday. Not even you can stop me.'

'What do you do on the other days?'

'I sit in a cell and try to forget.'

I gave him a puzzled look.

'Come on, Betty. You can't just show up out of the blue and expect something from me.'

'Why did you leave? How come you never got in touch?'

'I don't know.'

'But I want to know,' I said, thinking, I'm not budging until I find out what happened. Starting with the day he left.

'Yeah, yeah, you want to know everything, but you can't take the truth.'

'I've got plenty of time,' I said.

'It's not about time, it's about forgiveness.'

'I forgave you long ago. I had no choice.'

'We don't forgive anyone for silence, Betty. We just make our peace with it, and we do it alone, without the other person. We don't forgive, we accept. And we can accept a lot of shit, endless rivers of it. With alcohol, we can accept even more. I took you to school that day, packed my things and left. I didn't expect you to forgive me. I had no other option.'

The longer he spoke, the more it sounded like he was summarising some international blockbuster. Like he'd taken a story and turned it into his own. Love, crime, guilt, everything a bit overbaked. It was a legend, and it went back to his young days. Maybe he'd condensed his life into a version he could tell himself, his own existence a sequence of far-fetched bullet points. The story began in Bellegra, with his first girlfriend, Elena, whom everyone called Elli, except for his sister, who called her 'whore'. They were together a couple of years, true love, he'd thought, until she fell for someone else in town, an awful braggart, the son of an extremely powerful family.

He hadn't felt rage, only grief, which is why he packed his things and left. Like nearly everyone else, he went to Germany. He played in dance halls the length and breadth of the country, women following him wherever he went, or so he claimed. A combination of his melancholy and his accent, he said. They all fell in love with the cliché and he was out the door before things could get serious. It was a sad time, he said, he didn't even have fun. Ten years of hopping between beds and stages, and then Baden-Baden. A big ball, him in the orchestra wearing a borrowed smoking jacket, Elli in front of him wearing a red dress and lots of gold, too much gold. She was positively dripping, Ernesto said, with his dirty money. The braggart at her side had got fat. Anyone with eyes could see he was shady, a scumbag godfather, as Ernesto put it. He and Elli didn't exchange a word all evening, and that night, after losing all his money in the casino, he resolved to start over. With that in mind, he met my mother. She was standing behind the bar of a pub in Hamburg, where he was in the process of getting drunk.

'She looked like she needed rescuing,' Ernesto said, laughing for the first time. 'She actually believed that. That people can be rescued. In a pub, of all places! A sweet woman, your mother, romantic, but not the brightest.'

He stood up and left me alone again. The man going back into the taverna, the man I'd been pining for my whole life, was a stranger. I looked at the empty chair opposite me, at the spat-out husks, at the horizon darkening as if the sky had cast an infinite shadow.

Never before had I felt such a strong urge to defend my mother, to protect her from this sick world. Our relationship seemed to be reversing; for reasons I couldn't quite explain, I now owed her the things she'd never been able to give me. What he saw as stupidity was just insecurity, always had been. But where on earth was a sense of security supposed to come from? We have so little of anything inside us, everything's poured into us as we go along, and during this process, some people are lucky and others aren't. If luck is in short supply, we might develop nothing but a determination not to go under, but sometimes even that crumbles, sometimes our circumstances defeat us.

'At least she was smart enough to know what she wanted,' I said when Ernesto returned, placing the same round on the table.

He agreed. She was a bloody strong-willed woman, he said, but her will tended to outstrip her abilities.

'She was constantly disappointed in everyone,' he said. 'Constantly offended, your mother. That hurt look on her face all the time! You used to take the mickey out of her.'

I didn't remember. But then, this wasn't my story.

A few years later, Elli got in touch with him. They met in secret in various towns on his tour routes. I pictured seedy hotel rooms with toilets in the hallways and asbestos in the walls. His life had never been glamorous and a woman with a rich husband wasn't going to change that. He started talking about the gold again. Apparently her jewellery was reason enough to run off with her.

He recounted his legend as if I were a stranger in a bar. I recognised every phrase, every threadbare joke, every embellishment. I'd heard too many stories like this before. Behind every cliché there's an omission, an untruth, even if the narrator seems to be baring his soul. A soul is just another story, I thought, reduced to an anecdote.

When Elli's husband came after them, they had no choice but to flee. It wasn't about love for him, it was about honour, according to Ernesto, and honour brings out the savage side of men.

'There wasn't even a jetty here in those days,' Ernesto said. 'A dinghy took us the last few metres to the island. A godforsaken place. It was perfect.'

We looked towards the sea, at the port with its little concrete pier. I hadn't noticed that the storm had subsided and the sky was clearing.

'I felt bad about you,' he said. 'But I'd no choice.'

With a pat of my hand, he told me he'd been young. The worst of all excuses. And anyway, he'd been forty, as I reminded him now.

'Forty is young,' he said. 'You just don't realise it until you're seventy.'

I too only felt young in retrospect, but I already felt too feeble to cope with the unreasonable demands made by ageing.

'I couldn't contact you,' he continued. 'I couldn't trust anyone. And your mother – well, you know, your mother is your mother.'

I probably shouldn't have nodded at this juncture, but I did. To my shame, an old feeling washed over me and bonded me to him for a moment: the comforting feeling of not being alone with my mother.

'We were happy here. We thought nothing could happen to us. But her husband never stopped looking. Elli must have sensed it; the tiniest noise would make her jump. I don't think she slept through a single night. And then, on a midweek morning, it happened. Our visitor didn't even knock, he just appeared in the house. We'd never seen him before.'

Ernesto stood up and took a few steps towards the sea. I imagined him wading in deeper and deeper until he vanished entirely, until he went under, never to return. I wouldn't have stopped him, I'd have spared him a rescue attempt. But he just stood by the shore, his shoulders drooped and his head bowed. How little there was left of him. The body I used to throw my arms around was gone.

He came back, grabbed a handful of seeds and sat there nodding and chewing for a while before coming to the end of his story, the finale, which began with a gun aimed at his head. No such story is complete without a gun, of course.

The visitor told Elli to get dressed and go with him, to come home. But Elli refused, went into a panic and hurled herself at the man.

'It was a mistake,' Ernesto said with a portentous nod. 'But she died on the spot.' And Ernesto did what he was best at: he ran away. 'If I'd been thinking straight, I'd have let him put a bullet in me too.'

He never found out how they got Elli back to Italy, he said. What he did know was that it wasn't her who was supposed to die but him, he'd been the target, and they'd covered up the mistake. They used Ernesto's papers to get her corpse to Bellegra. In his hometown, he was identified by his sister, officially declared dead and then buried. To this day, he wondered how she'd pulled it off. You couldn't put anything past her, she'd always had a finger in every pie, but he still didn't know why she'd confirmed his death, whether she'd hoped it would keep him alive or she'd just wanted to put an end to the rumours and bad blood in Bellegra.

He'd been stuck here ever since, illegal, no papers, dead yet still alive. The worst thing, he said, was the never-ending living. The bottomless guilt.

'Everyone here blames me for her death,' he said. 'But they want nothing to do with it. They keep their mouths shut, and I keep mine shut too. They've frozen me out.'

He stared at the empty glasses and bottles in front of us.

'They've let me go thirsty too. I haven't been served a drink in ten years, but here they let me help myself from the fridge, at least, and Grigori heats up my rakomelo. The Albanian. Another castaway.'

He got up and went back inside. He'd return in a minute with yet another round. His story was told, the sun was at its zenith. Another beer and I'd crumple in my chair like a Swedish tourist.

What the hell kind of tale was that, I thought. Who comes up with that kind of shit? Tramps and nut-jobs. For years, I'd been providing a sympathetic ear to life's failures. I attracted them, lost souls and their stories, and then I could never get rid of them. But this had started out differently. Ernesto hadn't come looking for me, I'd sought him out. I'd run after him, so desperate to find him that I discovered him in other men. I'd been abandoned, had suffered like a wounded dog, yet I'd only ever hoped he was happy. There was no vengeance to my love. But it hadn't worked. I didn't need to believe his story to see that the whole happiness thing hadn't panned out.

Ernesto returned with two beers and wanted to drink to God. I refused. Not once in my life had I drunk to God, it felt silly. Swaying, he leaned across the table, brought his bottle up to mine and said, 'If it wasn't for God, I'd be a goner.'

Poor old God, I thought. Or did I say it out loud? He gave a strange, dry laugh.

'Can you believe it? God saved me, of all people.'

'No,' I said. 'I really can't believe it.'

'So, to God!'

We clinked glasses, because if you start arguing over toasts, you'll never get down to drinking, and I had to say it, as loudly and clearly as I could by this point: 'To God!'

That seemed to placate him, and he smiled.

'So where does God come into this story?' I asked.

'I'm staying at his place,' Ernesto answered, taking a deep gulp. 'I'm kind of his caretaker. I get fed there. Free board and lodging, as they say.'

The monastery was the only place that hadn't turned him away, he explained. Everyone else shut their doors in his face after Elli died. The restaurant where he'd worked hired a new cook, he couldn't get a beer in the tavernas. He made it through the first summer in a remote cove, but when autumn brought the first storms with it, he went up to the monks and asked for asylum.

'They're good men,' he said. 'And they make good ouzo, too.'

That's another way of disappearing: when all else fails, God. Life offers many escape routes, and it seemed Ernesto had tried them all.

I was exhausted: from the beer, from his story, from the fact that I hadn't featured in it. I was just a minor character in a minor scene. He didn't ask once how I was or what I'd been doing with my life, not even out of politeness. But then, what would I have had to say? I was neither a success story nor a tragedy.

'How long are you staying?' he asked, and I would've liked to say that I was on my way to the ferry, that I'd just popped by for a few unhelpful answers, and that now I had to shoot off, I really had to dash. But none of that was true. I had no idea how long I was going to stay. Martha and Kurt would be arriving in a couple of hours. I was stuck here.

'Friends of mine are joining me tonight,' I said.

Ernesto nodded.

'I know what you want to hear,' he said. 'But I can't give you what you want.'

'What is it you think I want?'

'Love.' With that, he stood up and skulked down the promenade to his motorbike.

I suspected he'd soon regret saying that because as he left me, I sat there like a kid, a drunk, forgotten kid he'd have to come back to.

I heard a car pull up behind me. A familiar voice from an open window said, 'Come on, I'll bring you home.'

Summoning my last ounce of strength, I stood up and got into Yannis's car.

'You look as if you've just lost a battle,' he said, laughing. 'The battle against beer and the sun.'

'I need a lie-down,' was all I could respond. I was already seeing stars, and they came from neither alcohol nor the sun.

'You tourists are an odd lot,' Yannis said. He began to whistle a tune, a famous Greek lullaby, he said, sung to every child in the country to send them to sleep.

***

I awoke to knocking at the door and a name being called, mine. The room was completely dark. I'd fallen asleep fully dressed, just collapsed into bed. I stood up and opened the door to Yannis, who was standing there with his sign. 'We need to get going,' he said.

I ran into the bathroom, splashed water on my face, rubbed toothpaste across my teeth and rinsed. Even a night can be a new day. I hadn't reached the end yet; the end is always ahead of us.

The ferry was about to dock. We could see it from the terrace, a twinkling behemoth headed towards land. It would smash the port to pieces if it decided not to stop.

We jumped into the car and drove through ghostly silence. The lights were on in the tavernas but there was no one around apart from the usual Swede slouched in his chair. The port, though, was swarming with cars, people, signs. A piped melody wafted from the ship's belly to shore and church bells started to peal. I'd never heard them before, and perhaps I only heard them now because I was thinking about God's caretaker. But they kept ringing louder and faster, chiming euphorically, while beside us, rockets blasted into the air, exploding in a riot of colour over the sea as the ferry ploughed towards the dock.

'What's going on?' I asked Yannis. I found the commotion slightly menacing, but he was beaming. 'Who's on the ferry?'

Yannis laughed at me and said, 'Christós Anésti.'

'Who?' I asked, and then I heard it all around me: 'Christós Anésti!' they called out to one another. Yannis put his arm around me.

'Jesus is risen!' I still didn't get it and he must have thought I was the dimmest woman he'd ever slept with, certainly the least God-fearing. Orthodox Easter had begun, Great Lent was over and the party was getting started just as the gangway crashed onto the concrete.

Typical, I thought, Martha always knows how to make an entrance. She and Kurt were the last to disembark, he with an arm across her shoulders, she holding him by the waist, steadying each step. Kurt's face was the colour of chalk; he was barely able to stand. I hurried towards the two of them, and Kurt vomited in greeting, depositing at my feet what little was left in his stomach after the crossing. The expression on his face as Martha dabbed his mouth suggested he himself was amazed he'd survived the journey. He'd survived so much over the last while, his life transformed into one furious feat of survival after another, and in spite of his appearance, in spite of all the horror, in spite of all the pity I felt, I was overjoyed to see him, more overjoyed and more moved than I could ever have imagined. I hugged him so tightly I nearly cut off his air supply.

'Yeah,' he gasped. 'It's good to see you too.'

***

We couldn't refuse. The table was laid for six. It sagged under the weight of soup, biscuits and dyed red eggs. Yannis's mother, who until now I'd only seen from a distance, hugged each of us, one after another. Resistance was futile. Such hospitality can render the most beautiful places in the world intolerable. You can't escape it, you rave about it when you get home, but the truth is, it's exhausting. It was one thing I secretly liked about Germany: no one there had ever forced me to eat with them. People there were happy enough to leave me to my fate.

Kurt, the first to take a seat, sank into his chair, possibly thinking it was better to die than to be rude.

When everyone was seated, Yannis went to get his father. It was the first time I'd seen him. He looked too young to be in his condition, still clearly the same man who had built this house with his own hands. Yannis pushed the wheelchair and oxygen machine over beside Kurt, and the two men nodded at each other in acknowledgment of their mutual decrepitude. I found it cheering rather than sad. How many years of friendship does it take, how many shared booze-fuelled, love-fuelled nights, how many argument-fuelled, sulk-fuelled days, for us to admit that we're damaged? How little time we take, how quickly we give up, feeling rebuffed, misunderstood, unloved. How quickly it all becomes too much hassle, too complicated. But in the end, age exposes the damage, and all we need to acknowledge it is a nod.

Yannis's mother ladled soup into the bowls. It looked like puke, and as soon as that sordid thought crossed my mind, it started to smell like puke too.

'Magiritsa,' Yannis said. 'The soup that breaks the Lenten fast.'

Had I fasted, I might have dug in like his mother, but it seemed that she was the only believer at the table.

His father sucked in air before drinking from the bowl. Kurt, too, seemed nervous about filling his empty stomach.

When Yannis explained how the soup was made, Martha also began to struggle.

'The head of a lamb and its entrails – liver, kidneys, heart, tongue, lungs – then loads of dill, loads of garlic, loads of lemon. The next day, you cover the leftover offal in caul fat, wrap it in intestines, form it into a roll and then grill it over the fire. It's called kokoretsi.'

Laughing, he filled our glasses to the rim. He'd earned it, he said, Lent had been tough –one whole week without Facebook – a revelation no one seemed to find amusing, least of all his mother, who turned to me with a look I'd seen on the faces of many mothers in the past. Behind the friendly front, I was being subjected to a ruthless scrutiny I knew I wouldn't withstand, nor did I want to.

Was I married, she asked.

Was it my age, the south or Jesus? The question was getting annoying, but as I sought to dodge it, Kurt made a noise so animalistic that everyone started. Martha jumped up and, not knowing what else to do, whacked him on the back. Meanwhile, he flailed his arms around until he eventually grabbed Yannis's father's oxygen mask. After a few deep inhalations, he calmed down. With a smile and a stiff bow of the head, he passed back the mask and said, 'Fantastic air, thank you.'

The two men nodded again and started taking turns on the machine, inhaling old men's dope. They sat beside each other companionably, looking at the sea, their soup going cold in front of them. They looked happier than the rest of us.

I glanced over at Martha, whose left eye glistened with the suppressed tears of exhaustion that were sure to burst out of her in a few days, or weeks at the most. She had a tight grip on herself, as usual, so tight that she was in danger of strangling herself. The journey here must have been nightmarish. I didn't know why Kurt was doing this to himself, what kind of euphoria, what surge of elation had come over him just before the end.

Yannis's mother gave us a red hard-boiled egg each and, holding hers aloft, instructed us to tap them against each other. Whoever's egg remained intact would have a year's good luck.

We reached across the middle of the table and knocked the eggs together, the shells making a dull sound as they cracked. Only one egg was left unscathed, and it was Kurt's. It was either cynical or very truthful, as fate always is. When I removed the shell and bit into my egg, I saw that it was greyish-green inside.

***

It had been a sleepless night. I'd churned up and sweated through my sheets, got up countless times and paced around. The flickering had returned to my eyes and I couldn't see a thing, my head like a prison cell with walls as thick as years. The last few days had robbed me of my childhood; I suddenly felt old. It was as if the thing that had been holding me all these years had broken in two. So this is what they mean when they say let bygones be bygones. Your story implodes, the identity you've cobbled together falls apart. I thumped the pillow until the sun came up, then I made a coffee and stepped out onto the terrace. The sea was as smooth as an egg.

Out of the neighbouring room came Martha, who'd fallen asleep on her chair so suddenly and deeply last night that no one had dared wake her. Yannis had carried her to bed, where, for the first time in my life, I had tucked her in and stroked her hair. We gazed across the bay just as we'd gazed across the valley a few days earlier. It felt like years ago.

'Well,' Martha said, 'no matter where we go, the view is outstanding.'

I fetched her a cup of coffee. We'd never been talkative first thing in the morning, and anyway, I wouldn't have known where to begin.

'How's he doing?' I asked after we'd finished our first cup.

'He's asleep,' she said. 'And whistling. It's like he's riddled with holes and the wind is howling through him. He sounds like a rickety old house.'

'What on earth possessed you to come here?'

'You should've seen him, Betty. He was hyper, could barely sit still. Then Francesca says to me, get him out of here. He wanted to get away from her too. Maybe it wasn't such a good idea, meeting again. Just desperate romanticism.'

What if it never stops, I thought. What a horrifying prospect. What if there's always someone we're yearning to see again, what if we're at death's door and we're still hoping.

'Plus he kept asking after you: Where's Betty, what's she doing, why isn't she here?'

'After me totalling his car?'

'He thinks it was stolen.'

'Why did you tell him that?'

'Because it's easier to be a victim than a loser. As far as he's concerned, everyone is to blame but him: women, friends, bosses, criminals, whoever. The main thing is he has someone to blame.'

'I wish I was like that. I wish I could see the world that way.' Martha emitted a low groan.

'Christ, what kind of plonk were we drinking last night?'

'There are painkillers in my handbag,' I said, gesturing towards my door.

Martha went inside and didn't return for a long time. Just as I was thinking she'd fallen back asleep, she reappeared on the terrace. She looked different, and not in a good way: vertical creases between her eyes, the corner of her mouth twitching. I looked at her enquiringly, and she very carefully placed something on the table between us.

'What's this?' she asked.

'That,' I said without looking at it, 'is a nine-millimetre Beretta.'

'And where did you get it? When did you start packing heat? It's not unheard of, I guess: some women carry guns in their bags instead of mascara. Different strokes for different folks and all that. Or instead of antidepressants. That makes sense too.'

'I found it,' I said as calmly as I could. Conversations that take place when there's a gun on the table should always proceed as calmly as possible. Even conversations between best friends, especially conversations between best friends.

'And tell me, where does one find a nine-millimetre Beretta these days?'

'I found it in front of Ernesto's house,' I said. 'I had to take it. There was nothing else for me to take.'

'Why couldn't you have taken a pebble, for God's sake? Or a handful of sand?'

'It wouldn't have been the same.'

What I meant was, they would have been meaningless. There's a big difference between taking something meaningless and taking something meaningful, something that has meaning in and of itself, something that isn't just loaded up with meaning, pumped full of your own sentimentality. I myself had gone through that phase of drinking bottles of rum, filling the empties with foreign sand and putting them on my shelf back home. It hadn't worked, I'd come to realise; it was just tacky.

'Damn right it wouldn't have been the same!' Martha snarled. 'It would have been perfectly normal!'

'I've no intention of using it, okay? I just took it.'

We were interrupted by the sound of whistling, terrible, terrifying whistling.

'What's all the shouting about, girls?' Kurt was standing on the terrace in his washed-out pyjamas.

I grabbed the pistol and let Martha do the explaining. After all, she'd started it.

'Nothing,' she said. 'We were just talking about Martha's new boyfriend.'

'Oh dear, some things never change, do they?' Kurt said. 'Women bickering about men. Listen, girls, it's a waste of time. We're not worth it.'

I nodded, the gun between my knees under the table. I heard footsteps behind me and leaned forwards even further, practically hugging the table legs.

'Smell that?' Yannis yelled. 'How good is it? They've been spit-roasting lamb down there for hours, really slowly, on a low flame. You've never eaten anything as delicious, I promise. It's the Resurrection!'

***

Honestly, he was fine, Kurt insisted, he was happy to sit by the sea for a while. We should go ahead and take the boat out without him. It would do us good, he said; Martha needed a little break from him, and anyway, you can't turn down an offer like that. Only he could. Never again would he set foot on a boat, he said, he wouldn't survive it. No offence.

Yannis dropped him off at the taverna and we drove on to the port. I think it was at this point that Martha realised we were stuck here. Her father had ended up on an island and was determined never to get on a boat again. We were trapped in a dying wish that wasn't our own and it was more responsibility than she could shoulder.

Where was the nearest hospital, she wanted to know, and when Yannis said that it was three islands over, around ninety minutes by ferry, she let out a little wail.

'And the nearest doctor?' she asked.

'At the hospital,' Yannis replied.

Martha refused to believe they didn't have a doctor here. Come off it, she said, there had to be a doctor of some description. But Yannis shook his head.

'We have a hospital on the island,' he said, 'but no equipment and no doctors. Just a nurse, aspirin and plasters. The scheme was axed three years ago, like everything else in Greece. If you have an accident here, you die.'

We knew that the accident had happened long ago, and Kurt knew it too. I found myself hoping he wasn't fully aware of what he was putting his daughter through.

Martha put her head on my shoulder and went quiet. She'd bent to his will, like a child. It might not have been smart, but it was understandable. We got out of the car, climbed into a little wooden boat and with a hefty yank, Yannis started the motor. I felt an unexpected rush of liberation as we pulled away from the island. We all exhaled at the same moment, a soft, collective on-board sigh. 'We'll just go for a quick spin,' he'd said. 'It'll do you a world of good, some time away from the old farts.'

As Yannis steered us around deserted bays, we tilted our heads back and tried to let the beauty soothe us, tried desperately not to think about anything, but we were inexperienced. In fact, not thinking about anything was an entirely new skill for us.

Yannis abruptly shut off the motor and started to undress, not in a languid, sexy way, but in a frantic, clumsy tearing-off of clothes.

'Sorry, need to piss,' he said and jumped into the sea.

A few seconds later, Martha leaned out the other side of the boat and threw up into the water.

'He's not that ugly,' I said when she raised her head again.

'I think I might be pregnant,' she said.

I'd heard her say this sentence so many times it had lost all credibility.

'I've been feeling weird for a few days now,' she said.

'You're not pregnant, you're just strung-out,' I said in an attempt to reassure her, but she didn't want to be reassured.

'No really, I think I'm pregnant.'

'Pregnant by who?'

'What are you talking about, who?'

'Your next try isn't for another two weeks,' I explained. Over the past year I'd learned to remember her doctor's appointments by furtively noting them down. My diary was full of events, birthdays and occasions I was trying to take an interest in because I didn't want to lose my few remaining friends.

'Believe it or not, Henning and I still sleep with each other from time to time. For no particular reason, no plan, no hopes,' Martha said.

'Sorry, I didn't know.'

'It's nothing to feel sorry about.'

'No, I'm sorry I asked about ... I didn't mean ...'

'I know you didn't.' She tipped her head back again. 'God, I feel weird. Think I need to get back on dry land. This isn't agreeing with me at all.'

We stayed sitting opposite each other; if I went to her side of the boat to hug her, we'd capsize. So we just stared at each other and kept the boat balanced. Martha looked tired, bone tired.

'How come no one ever lets me rescue them?' she asked.

'Because not everyone wants to be saved,' I said. 'All we can do is not hold it against them. Especially not Kurt.'

She nodded.

'What about Ernesto? Did you actually find him?'

There was no valid answer. He was here, but it wasn't the Ernesto I'd been searching for.

'Yeah,' I said. 'Kind of. We went drinking together yesterday.'

Martha could believe neither that he was still alive, nor that I could think of nothing better to do with him than go drinking.

'I think the policeman in Italy was right,' I said. 'About everything.'

I stared out across the sea, at its little, innocent waves, and realised that Yannis was nowhere to be seen. I stood up and called out his name, getting neither an answer nor an echo in response. Seeing as we were in a two-by-four-metre wooden boat and therefore couldn't run around in panic, we stayed rooted to the spot, scanning the water.

'What are you doing?' Martha asked as I started to strip.

'What do you think I'm doing? Or do you think I should wait and smoke a fag first?'

How could someone drown in water like this, I thought. Who goes missing while they're going for a piss? What kind of a horror film was this? What was I going to tell his parents?

The minute I'd finally got my clothes off, an almost hairless head emerged from the water, followed by an arm, and finally a cheeky grin. I wanted to knock it off his face.

Yannis climbed back into the boat and stretched out his right hand.

'Look,' he said. 'I brought you shells.'

***

The whole town smelled of roast lamb. A spit revolved in front of every restaurant, children chased each other through the streets, a joyous mess of families, couples, friends, strangers. By the time we arrived back at the taverna, Kurt wasn't alone either. He was playing backgammon, something Martha said she'd never seen him do before. The only games she remembered were drunken gin rummy evenings on the then-new three-piece suite. When I saw who he was playing with, I wasn't surprised in the least. Coincidence or fate, I'd never differentiated between the two. Things just take their course.

We joined their table and I introduced Ernesto to everyone while he nodded wordlessly and made his next move. I silently watched the fathers continue their game. I couldn't look Yannis or Martha in the eye. Their proximity to my history made me squirm. Too intimate, too voyeuristic, as if someone was peering into my festering past, into a pain that couldn't be shared, couldn't be communicated. Much as I'd secretly relished this pain from time to time, it was humiliating to have it sitting there in front of everyone now, a lonely old arsehole living out his days on the Aegean.

I was thankful for the bustle that ensued when obscene amounts of meat arrived at our table, followed by rice, potatoes, chips and tin jugs of wine. A feast was about to commence, and I was determined to celebrate it to the last drop, to the last bone and the last word, to celebrate as if it was both the climax and the end of the story.

All around us, people were kissing, embracing, singing, clinking glasses, yelling 'Yamas!' and 'Christós Anésti!' Today, for one day, they were all saved. Kurt smiled at his daughter, and when someone smiles like that, they don't need to say anything. I could see Martha flush, her confusion creeping under her skin. He was looking at her with so much love, like she was a new-born baby.

We all noticed it and averted our eyes, not wanting to intrude. We reached for the lamb, practically pounced on it. It used to be Ernesto who brought meat home for dinner. Seldom steak, never fillet. Instead, he would boil and fry tripe, tongue and brain,

187

or place braided intestines on the barbeque. I was six years old and a demon for innards. After he left, I never ate them again, until yesterday. Now I had to admit to myself that I used to eat it all just to please him. I'd wanted to learn the trombone, too, an impossible dream given my small dimensions. Instead I got a recorder, which I never touched. At the age of ten, I declared myself a fan of free jazz, a genre that, as I only discovered much later, I actually find unlistenable. I drank my first Italian red wine at the same age, not a sip but an entire glass. Needless to say, I loved wine too, because it made him laugh. Like father, like daughter, except that he wasn't my father and never would be.

Did he still listen to jazz, I asked, but Ernesto replied that the monks' chants were all the music he needed, and when I brought up his Italian pop songs, he just gave me an uncomprehending look. I realised it's possible to lose all of your memories.

On one side of me, Martha had her arm around her father, and on the other, Yannis shifted his chair a bit closer. Even stray cats were being cuddled that day. Ernesto's legs bounced nervously. Maybe he wanted to run away or maybe it was just a symptom, an aftereffect of something else, something old. Yannis filled our glasses again, and again I drank Martha's as well as my own; she was furtively sticking to water. At the other tables, people began to sing, and the taverna owner started making his way over to us, half-hobbling, half-dancing. Just then, Ernesto stood up without uttering a word, undressed and strolled naked into the sea.

'Nutter,' the taverna owner said. 'He's a sick man.' He waved his hand, as if stories and sick men could be swatted away like flies. It's a gesture made by landlords the world over, and for good reason. Stories and sick men need to be got rid of lest they infect the other patrons.

'Who wants ouzo?' he shouted, but it wasn't a question. Grigori was already standing behind him with a full tray. They drank with us, to us and to Jesus Christ, and again I drank Martha's.

'Christós Anésti!' I slurred. If things kept going as they were, I'd be an Orthodox convert by the end of the night.

'Stupidito,' Grigori whispered in my ear like a threat, and then he rumpled my hair, which I suppose was his way of telling me I was in over my head. For a moment, I felt like I belonged here, like this village was my life, because it had everything: a man I'd slept with but didn't love; a father I didn't talk to; a best friend who stayed the same no matter where we went; mates who plied me with drink; and a Kurt, who I hadn't known for long but who I hoped would stay around forever, though I knew better. A totally normal life, a life that suddenly seemed blessed. I'd experienced such moments before, but they were becoming increasingly rare.

'Who's the man?' Kurt asked, pointing towards the sea.

'Ernesto,' I said. 'We met yesterday. He's a hermit, lives up in the monastery.'

Out of the corner of my eye, I could see Martha staring at me. Whenever she'd witnessed me lying outright before, it had been to cover for someone else rather than myself. Until now, all my untruths had been muttered quietly, and I'd get tangled up in the simplest of sentences. Now, Kurt just nodded and said he'd like to give it a go too.

'What, now you want to go live in a monastery?' Martha asked.

'No, I want to try the water. Just my feet, I just want to dip my feet in the water.'

'All right then,' she said, heaving him out of his chair. Yannis jumped up quicker than I was able to in my current condition and helped from the other side.

With slow, careful steps, they made their way down to the sea. Only now, from a distance, did I notice that Kurt was as small as a child. His body had buckled into the dimensions of a boy.

Ernesto waded back towards them, ramrod straight and brawnier than I would've guessed. I tried to remember if I'd ever seen him naked before, and when not a single memory came to mind, I was horrified to note a pang of disappointment shoot through me. He took over from Martha, who bent down to take off Kurt's shoes. Even from behind, I could see the exertion, the joy when Kurt finally stood in the water in his bare feet, propped up by the two men.

Martha had taken off her shoes too, and now she was standing in front of her father, holding his hands. She was laughing, all of them were. Quiet, surprised laughter, no euphoria, not the wild, exaggerated laughter I'd encountered a few times before, the kind of laughter that always seemed rehearsed, fake. The stock scene of countless films: people peeling off their clothes, running into the sea naked and squealing, losing their minds with sheer joie de vivre and having sex, which of course never works in real life because the waves keep knocking you over and the cold shrinks everything.

I stayed in my chair and watched scenes layer themselves on top of each other, decades' worth of memories. I saw myself, sometimes hand in hand with others – people who weren't around any more, people I'd lost touch with – but mostly alone. So many shores on which I hadn't stayed and to which I'd never returned. But the scenes began to blot each other out and were replaced by what I saw in front of me: three people propping up a fourth person, an old man bathing his feet. In this single scene, I suddenly saw parts of myself, too many parts to gather together, they didn't cohere. It felt like the stages of my life were crashing in a romantic collision, in a harmoniousness I could barely stand. Don't bloody well start crying now, I told myself, but it was too late. I'd been blubbing more and more often over the last while. My defences were weakening, as though the energy I needed to hold back the tears was all used up. I hadn't yet grasped, and I certainly hadn't accepted, that instead of toughening up as I'd expected, I was becoming more and more porous. In my twenties, I'd floated, but now I was constantly on the verge of going under.

I was relieved when they turned around, waved to me and returned to the table with a hint of pride on their faces. Ernesto put his clothes back on, and Kurt said he couldn't remember the last time he'd put a single foot in the sea. Everything in his life seemed to be in the distant past, as if he'd given up living decades ago, losing himself instead in a routine of TV, beer and supermarkets. There are millions like him, people who value peace and quiet above all else, people who get stressed by anything unfamiliar, even the journey there. Why bother, when you can see everything on your screen in absolute, lethal safety? His smile was so thin that I guessed it was wistful. Wistfulness is a thin emotion, a hairline crack, and the smile never left his face again. Kurt looked around and regarded each one of us.

The taverna owner brought us biscuits, and when he yelled, 'It's on the house! Everything's on the house! Everything's on the Greeks!' Kurt roared with laughter for several seconds.

We ate the honey-coated treats until our mouths turned sticky, and then washed it all down with ouzo. Ernesto slammed his glass on the table, took a swig and a deep breath and started to sing, a familiar melody, a song that felt as if it was being injected into me, its effect immediate, my entire body warming as soon as I heard it.

Lasciatemi cantare
con la chitarra in mano
lasciatemi cantare
sono un italiano

Opposite him, Kurt cautiously bobbed his head until the third verse, when to our and no doubt his own surprise, he joined in, singing along to a summer hit that had tinkled its way into the collective unconscious more than thirty years ago. His eyes closed, he sang:

Lasciatemi cantare
con la chitarra in mano
lasciatemi cantare
una canzone piano

The fathers sang, their voices low and croaky, and while Martha was amused, I was so moved that I joined in, partly to distract myself, and partly so that later I could look back on a scene in which I featured as more than just a spectator. I sang myself into my own memory, filing it away under the heading 'Happiness' even as I was experiencing it.

Lasciatemi cantare
perché ne sono fiero
sono un italiano
un italiano vero.

We sang softly, with one voice, and when we got to the last 'italiano', Kurt slumped into his chair, his head flopping onto his chest, and the whistling started up again. For now, it was an even, steady sound, but it would soon become ominous. We watched him as if he were a child we didn't want to wake, as if we'd have to wrap him in a blanket and carry him to the car. He looked content.

'I'll drive you guys back,' Yannis said. But when I tried to stand up, Ernesto reached for my hand. This was no gentle stroke. He grabbed me roughly, his fingers gripping my wrist so tightly it hurt. It was a command, not a request.

'Let's play,' he ordered, pulling me back onto my chair.

Martha asked if I needed rescuing with a look we'd been exchanging in situations like this for decades now, a look we shot each other whenever someone came too close to us, whenever boundaries were crossed and we weren't quite sure if it was grounds for hope or fear.

Here it was both, as had often been the case recently. I was afraid of what I wished for. No one could help me here, no one could protect me.

They put Kurt on the back seat, his head still drooping as Yannis buckled him in. He was sleeping the sleep of the dead. The car crawled down the promenade, and only after it had disappeared around the corner did Ernesto and I look at each other.

'What do you want?' I asked.

'I want to show you something,' he said and stood up.

***

I was holding on tight to him but I felt no closeness, no affection or trust, just muscles, flesh and dry, old skin. Once, this body had given me something to hold on to, but now my hands slid right off. It wasn't just hard, it was cold. The twists in the road terrified me; he sped around each one as though he'd forgotten he wasn't alone. I supposed it had been a long time since he'd carried someone on the back of his motorbike. As we rode through the night, I could guess where he was taking me, and I knew that it wouldn't be pleasant, whatever it was he wanted to show me. For the first time, I felt afraid. Being afraid of a man I'd once trusted more than anyone else was disturbing, because it implicated me. Not trusting him any more meant I couldn't trust myself either. I no longer knew who we were or who I'd once loved. Soon his house would appear on the left-hand side, a good distance from the road, the hideout that hadn't kept him safe.

Pebbles and sand battered my calves as I screwed up my eyes against the wind. We skidded for the last few metres, and when he killed the engine, the silence seemed brutal. The little plot of land now felt like the battlefield it must have been to him. Ernesto didn't walk towards the house, but away from it.

'Come with me,' he said, taking my bag, and I followed him without replying. He stopped at a spot I was familiar with. A small hole in the ground where two days earlier something had been buried. Ernesto crouched down, picked up a handful of earth and let it trickle through his fingers. Then he reached into my bag and looked up at me. We stared at each other for so long that it began to feel as if nothing existed in the darkness apart from the whites of our eyes.

'It's the gun that killed Elli,' he said.

He'd found the pistol when he'd returned to his house the next day. It had been buried so sloppily that he couldn't miss it.

'It was no accident,' he said. 'It was a threat. And a summons.'

He'd left the gun lying there all these years, hoping the man would come back and finish what he'd been sent to do.

'Every morning I sit down in the house and wait for him. For him or someone else. I sit for hours just inside the door. For ten years, I've been sitting in that house, waiting for it all to be over. But no one ever came,' he said, looking back up at me. 'Until now.'

The man crouching in front of me had driven himself insane. He stood up.

'No,' I said, yet I let him take me by the hand. My body had been severed from my will. I moved in a direction I didn't want to take, as if I'd lost consciousness but kept trudging on regardless.

We entered the house. It was colder inside than outside.

'I'd offer you a whisky,' he said, 'but as you know, there's nothing here.'

He sat down on the bare floor as I remained standing, my arms crossed, until I felt myself starting to sway and grabbed a bedpost.

'No,' I said again. It felt as if our entire history was being tied up into a single syllable.

'I'm a wreck, Betty, a spineless old wreck. I can't do it. All these years, that gun's been lying there. I've picked it up so many times. Someday I'll have the guts, I thought, someday I won't be able to take it any more. Maybe I was waiting for you.'

I just kept shaking my head.

'Why else is all this happening now? Why are you here, why did you find me in the middle of nowhere?'

I didn't have a single answer. It felt as though none of the decisions that led me here had been my own, as though I'd been steered to this moment. As though there'd never been any intention behind my actions, or if there had, then this was it. To stand opposite him, with a loaded gun between us.

'There's only one policeman on the island,' he continued. 'I've been officially dead for ten years. I was buried long ago. No one will care.'

I walked towards him and looked at him sitting on the floor in front of me, the gun in his hand. A man looking to me for salvation.

'It'll look like I did it myself,' he said.

I bent down and my cheek grazed his, as if by accident, a moment of weakness. We said nothing; it was far too late now. I just took the hand that had never managed to pull the trigger. My hand was now big enough to hold his, I thought. How it had grown, this hand I didn't recognise. The hand of a woman I didn't know, cocking the gun.

Ernesto didn't close his eyes, he opened them wide and gaped into his empty house. I breathed in and breathed out, not feeling afraid any more, just cold. I lowered my arm. I wasn't going to let him bring me down with him for ever. My hand wasn't holding anything or anyone now. It had let everything go, was completely alone.

***

Strange noises in the trees and bushes, rustling everywhere, a cry in the distance, breathing close by, a shadow flitting past. I listened numbly, waiting for a gunshot. I'd have to walk for hours to reach the village, where they might still be singing and celebrating a resurrection. I was standing on a deserted island road, my bearings lost.

I wanted to run so I wouldn't have to think, run until I could hear nothing but my own footsteps, until I was nothing but breath. I couldn't let myself come to a standstill.

Was that a bang? Had I just heard the first shot? The second, the third? Was he emptying the magazine, or did he keep missing because he was too weak to hold his hand steady? Had I heard anything at all? Maybe tonight was the night I'd finally tip over into insanity. Maybe I was running straight into madness, I thought, and I kept on running until out of nowhere, I heard steps behind me – heavy ones, like someone treading in hobnail boots – and snorting. Someone was following me, but I didn't look behind me, didn't stop. I wouldn't show fear, never. Fear just makes everything worse. The steps kept getting closer, and when they were just a few metres away, I turned around.

We stared at each other. His eyes were coal-black and surrounded by a white coat. His muzzle was white too, as were his teeth, which practically glowed in the dark. I heard a scream that seemed to come from the sea but I realised was my own. Unperturbed, the donkey regarded me for some time before eventually trotting on. Trembling, I followed from a safe distance. When he stopped, I stopped. When he moved, I moved. It was a game, but it was a long time since I'd played anything and I didn't understand what the aim was. Only when I kept walking and he remained motionless did I realise that the donkey was waiting for me, that this was the goal: to get me to catch up with him and accept his invitation. If he won my trust, he won the game.

When I joined him by his side, he grunted, and I felt like grunting too, but instead I stroked his neck, his dry, old coat. He kept tossing his head back until finally I mounted, and victorious, he carried me across the island.

***

Yannis was sitting on the terrace, watching the night go by. He'd been waiting for me for hours, he said. He'd been worried. He was worried about all of us. Two women, two old men, it wasn't good, he said.

'I like you,' he said, 'but you're all batshit. And your pal Ernesto, he's the worst. Not only is he batshit, he's sad too. And that combination turns people into loose cannons. You need to steer clear of sadness and madness. Men like him leave nothing but misery in their wake. They're poison.'

'Don't worry,' I said, a sentence that had never reassured anyone, at least not when it came out of my mouth.

'How did you get back?' he asked.

'Ernesto gave me a ride.'

He nodded.

'And here was me thinking I'd seen a donkey.'

Above the sea, the darkness began to lift, but I wasn't holding out any hope that the night's events would turn out to be a dream.

'You look like you'd rather be alone,' Yannis said, waiting in vain for me to protest before going inside.

I wondered for a moment whether it was the tourist industry that had made him so sensitive, or whether he'd had a difficult childhood. Then I looked out again at the bay, a view that had at first seemed like a revelation, back before I learned that revelations can take away your memories. I wanted to spit on the beauty down there, pretending to be so innocent. I wanted to spit on myself for believing for so long that you can't free yourself from your own history. Something inside me hurt, because something was over, and something had awoken, something was about to begin. I looked at the hands I'd managed to save from doing harm: they lay there completely still. When I raised them as if to bid a final farewell, I heard the door open behind me. Martha stumbled half-asleep out of my room. 'Sorry,' she said. 'I slept in your bed. I couldn't take it any more, the whistling.'

We looked at each other and couldn't look away, because we both heard it: nothing. No whistling. Just silence. The kind of silence that precedes a solar eclipse, when animals hush and the wind subsides, when everything goes quiet and a moment later, the earth darkens.

A noiseless scream surged through Martha. She pulled open the door of Kurt's room, ran inside and her scream found a sound. It wasn't piercing, wasn't even loud. It came from so deep down inside her that it sounded as if she was being rent in two.

I wanted to run after her but my body felt too heavy to carry. I hauled myself out of my chair and planted one foot in front of the other until I was in the room. The walls seemed to be shaking and Martha was standing in front of the bed, where Kurt looked as if he'd been laid out.

'Call a doctor!' she shouted, and her legs buckled beneath her.

His mouth was slightly open, his arms stretched out on top of the duvet. He looked at peace.

'He's smiling,' said Martha. 'Isn't he?'

'Yes, he is,' I said.

What she hadn't seen, not yet, was the empty bottle of ouzo under the bed and the bottle of pills on the bedside table.

I looked down at Kurt, feeling nothing. My emotions lay dormant; it often took them days to arrive. It had long been a source of shame to me, but never more so than now. I watched Martha crouch by the bed and reach for Kurt's hand, which was probably still warm. I watched myself stand behind her, rubbing her shoulders but wanting to hold her, to pull her away into a world in which none of this had happened.

The peculiar, unmistakable, indescribable smell of an extinguished life hung in the room. No other smell radiates such peace, has such a narcotic effect. Beneath my hands, I felt Martha's breathing slow down. She put her head on the edge of the bed and I stroked her hair. Time had stopped existing; there was just this moment putting everything else on pause.

As I stood there, I spotted a scribbled note on the table. I squeezed Martha's hand – I'd squeeze it for the rest of our lives – and said, 'Look, Martha, a letter.'

My darling Martha,
There's only one thing in my life I'm proud of, and that's you.
I want to go before it starts to hurt. Promise me you won't
hurt either.
You know I'll keep an eye on you.
I have to go now.
I'll have my arms around you forever.
Dad

PS: Thank you for the wonderful past few days. Next time,
let's start earlier.
PS 2: You're getting stronger and stronger. You can do it, all
of it.
PS 3: I love you.
PS 4: My insurance number: 612/654354-G
PS 5: Name your son Kurt, okay? He'll be a better Kurt than
I was.
PS 6: Give Betty my love. Tell her she must never marry.
She'd be wasted on just one man.
PS 7: Drink your next ouzo to me, always to me.

So long, my beautiful daughter. So long!

Translator's Note

I first encountered Betty, Martha and Kurt, the sardonic, intractable protagonists of *Daughters*, at HAM.LIT, Hamburg's annual festival of contemporary German literature and music, in February 2018. A large crowd had gathered in the darkened auditorium of a nightclub, bottles of beer in hand, to hear Lucy Fricke read from her new novel for the first time. Lucy chose one of the book's early scenes: Betty, Martha and Kurt bickering about feminism, money and the perils of dating men with tattoos as they splutter down the autobahn towards a euthanasia clinic in Switzerland. It didn't take long for the audience's reverent hush to dissolve into gales of laughter at the gallows humour. Glancing at the people creasing up around me, I thought about how I'd love to share this uproarious side of German literature, so underrepresented in the English-speaking book market, with readers back home. I bought the book right after the festival, and reading – or rather devouring – strengthened my desire to share this wise and witty tale with readers outside Germany. The question was, would I be able to find a publisher willing to take a risk on a German novel that dared to be funny? Imagine my delight when around a year later, I received an email from V&Q Books telling me they had secured the translation rights for *Daughters* and would like me to do the honours.

Once the initial elation subsided, though, the self-doubt began to creep in. Humour is widely considered one of the most difficult things to translate. Would someone as tragically unfunny as myself be able to make the novel funny in English? I pictured my translation as a bad stand-up comedian delivering dud one-liners to a heckling audience. Rereading the novel only deepened my trepidation as I realised how much of the humour is rooted in a specifically German context. What was I going to do with the refences to the dive bars of Hamburg's St Pauli, the gentrification of Berlin's Kreuzberg and the fashion choices of the residents of Marzahn? What about the gentle mocking of the postwar Germans' romantic image of Italy and Greece? How would I translate the joke about becoming a *Tussi*, a derogatory term for a certain kind of aspirational German woman for which I have never been able to find a satisfactory English equivalent? How would I manage the allusions to the bland department store Karstadt and the talk-show host Sandra Maischberger? Would English-speaking readers understand the various sociocultural connotations of beer, schnapps and Aperol Spritzes? Should I provide glosses to help them get the punchlines? No, that wouldn't work; everyone knows jokes stop being funny when you start explaining them. And then there was the wordplay and neologisms (such as Betty's characterisation of the tightly wound Martha as a *Linksheulerin*, someone who only cries out of her left eye), not to mention Kurt's ridiculous northern German pet names for his daughter. Every time I came across another instance of Lucy's linguistic inventiveness, I gulped.

But as Betty points out, sometimes when a difficult journey lies ahead, you just have to say, 'Let's go.' So I got going, in the hope that I would figure out how to circumnavigate the roadblocks as I went along. And once I did start translating, I found the voices of Lucy's characters so strong, so authentic and so true to my own experience that the cultural specificities no longer seemed so important. Betty and Martha's midlife worries about ailing parents, stalled careers, ticking biological clocks and romantic disappointments echoed those of friends of mine back home in Ireland. Not only that, but Betty and Martha *talk* the way so many women I know talk. The characters' resilience and refusal to lose their sense of humour, no matter what life throws at them, reminds me of dear friends scattered all over the world. Once I had found the characters' voices, I realised that the tone and rhythm of their language is often as integral to the humour as the semantic content; after all, any comedian will tell you it's all in the delivery. So I focused on getting these aspects right, and solutions to the translation challenges outlined above began to present themselves. Sometimes I "domesticated" the cultural references to make them relatable to non-German readers – so the allusion to the fashion of Marzahn became a line about a trailer park, for example – but very often I found that wasn't necessary; the rhythm of the repartee is funny, I think, even if you are not intimately familiar with the culture in which the jokes are rooted. On a rare occasion, I reluctantly opted to let a joke go, feeling that would be truer to the spirit of Lucy's novel than forcing the point.

For all that I was concerned to make English-speaking readers laugh, I hope I have also managed to capture the sadness, longing and hope at the core of this story. I have reread the novel countless times by now, yet certain scenes still bring tears to (both) my eyes. *Daughters* is far more than a collection of dark jokes. At its heart, it is a moving exploration of ageing, loss, family and the consolations of getting drunk with an old friend – themes that will surely resonate with readers far beyond Germany's borders.

Sinéad Crowe, May 2020